Wigan is Wonderful

Julian Simpson

UKA PRESS

UKA Press, 55 Elmsdale Road, Walthamstow, London, E17 6PN, UK
UKA Press, Olympiaweg 102-hs, 1076 XG, Amsterdam, Holland
UKA Press, Anderson St, 108, 2-5-22 Shida, Shizuoka 426, Japan

2 4 6 8 10 9 7 5 3 1

First published in Great Britain in 2007 by
UKA Press, 55 Elmsdale Road, Walthamstow, London, E17 6PN

www.ukapress.com

A CIP catalogue record for this book is available from the British Library

ISBN: 1-905796-06-4 978-1-905796-06-9

Printed in the United Kingdom

Cover design by Peter J. Merrigan

Cover photograph by Paul Bowen Simpson

Edited and prepared for print by John F Griffiths
(www.e-griff.com)

For the boys,
and Wigan,
which truly is wonderful.

Wigan is Wonderful

Wigan is wonderful, thought Jason. Where else in the country, in the whole fucking world, could you be in a strange house, kneeling on the living room floor, banging the arse off some bird whose name you forgot the moment she told you because you were so pissed? Jason knew how he'd got here, he just wasn't too sure where 'here' was. He was still marvelling at how it had all happened and that was making the details a little blurry. One minute he'd been standing in the taxi rank arguing with the girl in question that her house wasn't on his route home, the next thing he knew they were chewing each other's faces off on the back seat. And now her skirt was pulled up around her waist while her parents snored away loudly upstairs. He couldn't stop smiling. God knows how old she is, her face is hidden behind a veil of permed blonde hair that jumps up every now and then when he thrusts. He can't really remember what she looks like and at this moment he doesn't even care. He's not had this happen for a while, pulling when he didn't mean to. He'd just been out round town, necking beer after beer with his mates, not even trying it on really. He remembers dancing for a while and some bird taking exception to him grabbing her arse, but the time between then and now is lost forever in the recesses of his mind. The last tangible memory he has since the taxi is when they'd started on the couch and he'd lifted up her skirt to go down on her. She'd held his head down for as long as he could take while she ground her hips against his face and then begged him to bite her neck. She wanted a mark, she said, a big fucking mark. And he couldn't even remember her name. His smile turned into a grin as he grabbed her harder and the next thing he knew he couldn't stop laughing.

Denise sat back on the burn-hole cratered brown sofa and inhaled deeply. The room was filled with blue smoke that hung in the air like vast, undulating blankets, making her vision even more hazy. Her head was swimming as all the substances inside her body made their way through her bloodstream. There was music playing somewhere, but it sounded muted inside her head. There were other people, but she couldn't focus on any of the figures moving around in front of her. She felt the sofa move as someone fell next to her and removed the joint from her hand. She turned and for a brief moment saw his face before it blurred away in front of her eyes. She felt like she was going to be sick, but when she tried to stand she realised she couldn't. It was as though her legs were not attached to the rest of her anymore. Pins and needles ran through her entire body and while her feet felt heavy on the floor, her legs were fluid. She remembered how she had arrived at the flat with Dan, her boyfriend, how he had helped her up the flights of stairs in the tower block. But she didn't know where he was now and she was beginning to lose the battle with the wrenching sensation emanating from her stomach.

Suddenly she felt arms lifting her up from the sofa, dragging her through another room as the fluid inside her began to rise and she saw it spray out before her as the bathroom door was flung open and she fell towards the toilet. She made a grab for the porcelain and tried to aim into the bowl, retching even harder as she saw the vomit already inside. When there was no more to come, she turned and saw that whoever had helped her into the room was no longer there. She leaned against the wall and passed out.

'Drink up gentlemen!'

'Been watching 'tics tonight Frank?'

'Aye, down at JJB.'

'What were score in end? Last I heard it were two nil.'

'Three bloody nil in end. Waste o' bloody time. That manager wants his head seeing to, I've never seen such a bloody shower in all me life.'

'Three nil at home, that's sacrilege that.'

'It's bloody scandalous is what it is. The season's only just started and we're already getting beat. And that forward, the new lad, couldn't score in a bloody brothel. No heart, that's trouble. No bloody heart.'

Mark can hear his father talking in the other bar, but his eyes and his thoughts are firmly fixed on the main function room where the DJ box is being packed away in the far corner as the hen night winds down. He's been working as a glass collector in the Parish Hall for nearly six months now and hen nights and birthdays and wedding anniversaries are a regular occurrence. He looks forward to hen nights the most though, when the women get totally plastered away from their husbands and boyfriends and etiquette goes out the window. He's picked up nearly a tenner in tips as purse strings dangle looser for a night.

By law, he's not supposed to sell drinks, he's not old enough, but John, the bar manager, lets him do it tonight as they're understaffed. The men who work behind the bar do so voluntarily, with drinks making up their wages. For long periods Mark is left on his own as John goes into the members' lounge on his right to talk to some people he knows, sitting down and smoking a cigar. But the night is coming to a close, 'last orders' is being called and John makes his way around the tables, picking up the odd empty glass here and there.

Mark stands behind the lager pump and watches the women dancing without music, some singing off in a corner, the older ones slowly finishing their drinks or putting on their coats and saying goodbye to the merry girl by the door, who props up her back with one hand and holds a half empty wine glass in the other. Mark's eyes don't leave her bulging stomach as she laughs with the departing women. He knows the girl, she's called Stacey and lives over the road from him. He can't take his mind off how she'd grabbed his arse when he'd been crossing the dance floor earlier with the green glass carrier heavy in his hand. The bump fascinates him and for a brief second he feels as though her eyes meet his as she turns and accepts a cigarette from the girl next to her. He keeps on watching as she lights up and takes another drink, before being led over to some older women by a table at the far side of the hall. When he realises she isn't going to look back again he turns and sees his dad waiting at the bar.

'Time gents please!'

'Sneak us a pint while he's not looking lad.'

'Dad I can't do that. I'll get sacked.'

'No you won't. Come on, now, while his back's turned. He's a friend of mine anyway, if he sees you I'll sort it out.'

'All right Dad.' Mark pours the pint, shielding it with his body, then passing it to his dad.

'There's a good lad.'

John's voice calls, 'Mark, stop nattering away you lazy bugger! Frank stop distracting your lad, he's supposed to be bloody working for me, not propping up the other side of the bar.'

'Go on lad, get yourself collecting some glasses, here's fifty pence for that pint.'

'Oh, cheers Dad.'

'Mark, get your arse round there and get some bloody glasses!'

'Look what you've done to me neck, me mam's gonna fucking kill me.'

'What?' asked Jason, his eyes having trouble focusing on what was happening and his head taking an age to work out where the hell he was.

'Look at it, how am I going to hide this?' she said, and as Jason's eyes opened more fully and he saw the girl leaning over him, quick bursts of memory hit his brain along with his hangover. She turned her head and pointed to her neck and he saw that she had four large love-bites up one side, running from near her collar-bone almost to her jaw. The bigger ones were connected by lighter coloured bruises and made that part of her neck nearly completely black, as though she had been hit by a cricket bat.

'Fuck.' Was all he could say.

'Fuck,' she said. 'What am I going to tell me mam?'

'I don't know, you asked me to do it.'

'Well you've got to go, she'll be up any minute.'

'Who will?'

'Me mam.'

Finally her words started to connect with something in Jason's head and he was filled with an instinctive survival response. He sat up and found he was naked. He had a crick in his neck from where he had been lying, but he was sure she hadn't slept in the bed with him, it was far too small. The room seemed like it belonged to a little kid, a younger brother or sister. There were teddy bears on the wallpaper next to his head and the bed he was in could only belong to a smaller person.

'Come on, get your clothes on.' Jason took his boxers from her and stood up to put them and the rest of his clothes on. A searing pain burned along the top of his head the minute he found his feet and he dizzily fell onto the bed again. 'Jesus, are you still pissed?' she said.

'Fuck,' said Jason, leaning his head back onto the pillow.

'Oh my God, I'll go and phone you a taxi, you've got to get out of here.'

Denise woke up feeling even worse than she had the night before. She had no idea where she was, but she was on her side. She tried to blink her eyes open but her lids felt stuck together. Eventually she looked across the floor and saw the assortment of socks and CDs scattered across the carpet. Her back hurt like hell and she uncurled herself from the foetal position she was lying in. There was a naked light bulb shining directly above her and the sun was visible through an open window over a dishevelled bed to her left. Whose bedroom was this and how had she got in here?

She wasn't nearly ready to deal with the pain inside her head, which felt as though someone had started a small fire behind her eyes, and she let out a groan. She sat up, but couldn't stretch her legs out at first and it took her a moment to realise her knickers were around her knees. She looked around quickly but couldn't see anyone in the room with her. She reached between her legs and felt the flaky substance there.

'Oh God,' she said. She tried to run through the events of last night but she couldn't remember anything in any real order. She knew she'd been pissed and stoned and she vaguely remembered throwing up, but everything else was a blur. Looking down and patting her body she discovered that the rest of her clothes were intact and she still had her shoes on. Where the fuck was Dan? She lifted her hand to her nose and smelled her fingers, already knowing what was on them before she did so. Using what energy she could muster she pulled her underwear back up and ran out of the room, not registering if anyone else was in the flat or not, just wanting to leave and trying not to vomit as she clip-clopped down the concrete steps to the street below.

He is in love with her. She does not know this, just like she doesn't know that he watches her and thinks about her nearly all the time. He has seen her getting undressed hundreds of times, it is an almost nightly ritual and he will break off any prior engagement to be in his room with the lights off late at night so he can watch her. He hopes that she knows he is watching, that she strips just for him, but he doesn't think it is true. She's just careless at closing the curtains that's all. He has felt like this before, back when he was ten years old. No one had ever told him heartache could be inflicted in primary school. She was the most gorgeous girl in the class. Blonde hair in thick plaited pigtails, sparkling blue eyes, always immaculately turned out in pretty dresses and shiny shoes. She was clever, good at sports and popular. And she was his girlfriend. Rose – that was her name. God knows where she was now or what she was doing. Probably doing well in school, probably nothing like the virginal vision he holds in his head, where she is standing at the school gates one minute, racing around the playground the next, her hair bouncing around behind her, her eyes beaming, her laugh riveting.

The school had organised a bird-watching holiday in the Lake District and he had gone on it. He wasn't all that interested in birds, but the teachers had said it would be fun, something different. Five whole days away from parents, away from his brother and sister, but unfortunately, away from Rose. He had thought about her nearly every day. The idea of going somewhere new had been exciting at first, and he could hardly believe it when his mum had said yes and signed the form. It didn't even matter that none of his best friends were going, but he had missed her in a way he hadn't thought possible. Almost the moment they had arrived he had wanted to go home, and it was five long days until he was back and then a whole weekend until school. He had spent most of the time in bed, his mum moaning about him not going out in the sun. And then, back in school, Rose had told him in their first lesson back together that she fancied Stuart Gross and wanted to be with him instead. She had looked at him with kind, sincere eyes, not wanting to hurt him, asking if he was okay. He'd said scornfully, 'What do you want me to do, cry?' But he had. The minute playtime kicked in and everyone went outside, he had gone straight around the back of the canteen and bawled his eyes out. The pain with Stacey isn't as bad because he makes himself remember that she is out of his league. In the back of his mind he knows that he can never have her, although it doesn't make him want her any less. He always wanted a girl next door, but he is happy to fantasise instead about the one over the road. He is fifteen and she is nineteen and she has always gone out with boys very different to him. He knows she would not look at him twice. He stands by the road, his arm over next door's car, with what he hopes is his best film star look. But the effort is wasted. She looks at him briefly, smiles and even says hi, before swaying off down the road. Off to see *him* probably, her future husband, to tell him all about her hen do over a couple more drinks and continue last night's feeling.

'Look at that, I'm not kidding. Some men are so fucking stupid. They slave away in a factory on twelve hour shifts and think their wives are just innocently wandering around the park pushing the pram.'

'Jay, that's what they are doing.'

'That's what they're doing now, but you just need to be a little bit persuasive. All they need is one little push in the right direction and they're putty in your hands, I'm telling you.'

'And how would you know?'

'Because I've experienced it first hand, that's how I know.'

'As if you have.'

'I'm telling you there's no feeling like banging a woman that belongs to someone else, no feeling in the world. I've had a woman spread out on her back screaming away while her kid is screaming its head off in the next room.'

'Doesn't that distract you?'

'No way, it makes you remember what she is, that she's got a kid and a husband and that she's sick of it, bored to death with it all and she wants you to fuck her brains out. And so you fuck her brains out, she gets fucked and her husband comes home too tired anyway and gets his dinner fresh on the table from a smiling wife. Everyone's happy.'

'Not everyone. The husbands wouldn't be happy if they ever found out.'

'Well I'm not going to tell them. And who else is going to? Not the wife, she's shit scared now, that's why she has dinner on the table the minute he gets back. It amazes me they never notice anything. They're so dumb these blokes. They come home tired from work, tired with life and think the wife's happy because they provide the money. Maybe they do, but I provide whatever else they need.'

'Speaking of what we need, when are we getting some draw for the party tonight?'

'This afternoon, I had a word with Tariq.'

'Who's Tariq?'

'Dan's mate. His dad owns the Post Office at the top of

Enfield Street.'

'What, the place where we got this beer?'

'Yeh. He told me all about this guy who lives in one of those blocks of flats in Scholes, says he can get us whatever we need, whenever we need it.'

'What's his name?'

'Who?'

'The guy who we get the gear from.'

'John, I think.'

'You think? We can't just go wandering around Scholes and not know what we're doing, it's like gun city round there.'

'Don't worry, Tariq said everything will be fine.'

'And you trust a Paki?'

'It'll be fine. Dan knows him and I've known Dan long enough not to think he'll fuck us over. He's going to have a word today and tell him we're going round.'

'Good job we're drinking before we go. Pass us the can.'

She takes a shower but she still can't get the dirt off. It's as though the filth is inside her, tainting her from her core. She's washed herself once already but it doesn't make any difference. She scrubs between her legs as the water cascades down her body, trying to wash away the idea as much as the physical remains. She has no memory of what has happened, but she knows that it has.

Her mind races as she tries to think what to do next, where she can turn now. Her knickers were around her knees when she woke up, dried spunk was between her legs, and she has no idea how it happened. She retches again, but there's nothing left inside her anymore. Maybe it's started already. Maybe it's begun so soon. Her mum hadn't even asked where she'd been as she knew she'd gone out with Dan. It's taken eight months but she finally trusts her with a lad. She even likes him. For the first time in her life Denise wasn't asked what happened the night before, what she'd done and who with. Salt water washes down her face with the soap.

Later, she stares at the mock Tudor shop fronts in town and

although she's there with two others she has never felt so alone. She can talk tough with them and drink and have a laugh, but there is not one among them she can discuss her fears with, or the fact that if what she thinks is right, she has no idea who the father is.

Dan and Tariq come over and he even puts his arm around her. She never thought she would be like this, never thought she would find a bloke whose arm she would want to have around her in public, in front of her mates. She relishes it now though, sees their jealousy at what she has, a proper boyfriend. He works in Next and always looks good. He is twenty-one, four years older than her, and always buys her drinks when they go out.

'You're looking good Denise,' says Tariq.

'Keep your eyes to yourself, you,' says Dan.

She loves this too, his mock jealousy, the attention Tariq pays her is welcomed because it brings out the best in him. She is careful not to overstep the mark though. Dan has a temper when he wants to.

'As if I'd ever look at you anyway,' she says, making Dan smile. She sits there and laughs when the boys come over, trying all over again, terrified that not one of them will ever touch her if they find out.

Messing about on BMX's, racing around the old dirt track in the woods, taking the jumps at speed and hanging on for dear life, he is still thinking about her, wondering if he'll ever meet a girl like that, get her in the family way, settle down. One of his mates has already done it and he says it's like a warm, wet tunnel. He told them all one night when they were sitting round with cigarettes pilfered from many mothers' untended packets and bottles of cider, how girls moaned when you did this or that to them, and how her hand had felt even better than his own. They all listened intently, taking nervous sips from their drinks, not wanting to miss a thing, imagining they had been there instead of him and thinking what a lucky bastard he was.

Mark doesn't know whether what he was told was true or not,

but he didn't dare question the validity of the story – he is still a virgin, a baby. He's kissed a girl before, but he was drunk and now the memory isn't so vivid. He no longer remembers what it tastes like, but he knows he wants to feel it again. He wonders when his first time will be, who it will be with. He wishes it could be with Stacey, but he consigns those thoughts to daydreams. She's getting married for God's sake. He still can't stop thinking about her though, her hair dyed almost white, with dark bits near her head. Her hair is dead straight and hangs down past her shoulders, not like his sister who uses about ten tons of hair spray to get it sticking up straight at the front. Most of the girls at school have it like that too, long, permed hair with big curving fringes lifted high above their foreheads. Stacey's is nothing like that, perfect in its straightness and angelic in its colour.

They take a ball down to the school field later on and have a kick about, whistling at some girls as they walk past the iron fence. The girls are a lot older than they are, but they whistle anyway and cheer when one lifts her top and flashes them.

'So are you coming down tonight then?'

'Where to?'

'Alexandra Park. There's a couple of girls from school going and they're all well dirty.'

'Where do we get beer from though?'

'Usual place, the Post Office. They'll serve anyone in there.'

'What time?'

'Half seven?'

'Nice one.'

The blocks of flats at Scholes are intimidating when you stand close up. From a distance, on the very edge of the town centre, they just look like big concrete piles set into grassy verges, painted in different colours almost as an afterthought – your average council-inspired housing venture, about fifteen storeys high, with lines of rainbow washing hanging out on the balconies. But when you get near, you can see all the concrete surrounding them, as though a disease is spreading from the top floor, down the towers and coursing outwards from the bottom, spreading the filth like fire along the ground. Up close the greenery is littered by smashed bottles, plastic bags, empty fag packets, rusty car and bike parts and popped footballs – an ash pit of half-life. No cars are in the car parks, just a couple of shopping trolleys and a ripped up tyre. But it's where you have to go on a drug run, whether you're looking for hard or soft, this is the main outlet, the supermarket of mind-altering substances, each tower block containing the possibility of a score. Jason is following Tariq's instructions about which one to go to and he and Johnny walk across the cracked concrete car park towards the steps leading upstairs. A man's voice calls out to them before they make it and they turn to see a black bloke riding a bike towards them. 'What you after boys?'

'Weed,' says Jason.

The guy stops his bike near them and gives them a good going over with his eyes. 'How much you want?'

'Just a quarter,' says Jason, beginning to wonder how to handle this situation. The guy looks suspicious of them, but is it a ploy, is he a copper in disguise trying to sting them, or does he think that they are coppers with the situation reversed?

'Give us your money,' he says at last. 'Look after my bike, I'd better go up on my own, there's been a few raids round here recently.'

'We know the guy,' says Johnny. 'We're mates of Tariq and he told us to see John.' Jason thinks it might be a bad idea, this guy might not even know John and competition breeds contempt. They're lucky though. It's John they're going to see.

'Come up then,' he says, leaning his bike against the side wall near the steps.

The stairs are dark and winding and smell of piss. There are supposed to be light bulbs lighting the way, but they were all smashed or nicked a long time ago. Jason isn't sure about this: Tariq told them everything would be okay, but that was before this new bloke got involved. There's not a lot he can do though, just follow him up the stairs, his stomach churning as he prays it'll be all right and nothing bad will happen. You could disappear around here and no one would have a clue. Four flights up and they suddenly stop in front of a green door. The paint is cracked and the wood looks flimsy, but if this is John's place, Jason can't imagine them having problems with burglars. The black guy turns to look at them before knocking on the door and Jason hopes he doesn't see the sweat forming on his forehead. It's not even slightly hot in the stairwell, but Jason feels the most uncomfortable he's ever felt in his life. A muted voice says something from behind the door.

'It's me.'

A girl opens the door slightly and peers out at them. She mumbles a hello to the bloke, closes the door, unclasps the chain and opens it properly. Jason turns to Johnny in the hope he looks a bit more certain about all this, but he doesn't, and they all walk into the flat. Inside the place looks a mess and the girl slumps next to three blokes sitting on a brown sofa watching TV. The room is filled with smoke and while the occupants of the sofa hardly move, a small bull mastiff makes its way over to Jason and sniffs his leg. Jason knows all about how dogs can sense fear and he tries to contain his anxiety, but it's hard enough in this situation as it is without a man-eater of a dog taking an interest in him. He tries not to move, other than wiping the swiftly gathering sweat from his forehead, and is grateful when another bloke appears from the kitchen at the far end of the room and calls the dog to him. It sniffs its way past the people on the sofa before retreating into the kitchen behind its master. Breathing in the overpowering odour of cannabis, Jason hopes the dog is as stoned as everybody else.

'You Jason?' says the bloke, who Jason recognises as John, leaning against the opening of the kitchen, almost obscuring the assortment of tattoos on his right arm. Jason has seen John before, but never this close and never in this sort of situation. He has a reputation as one of the few people who wouldn't just see you beaten up if he took a dislike to you, but could get rid of you once and for all.

'Yeh,' Jason manages to say. The black guy makes his way

over to John and says something to him quietly. John, who Jason reckons is somewhere in his mid-twenties, nods. Jason looks at those arranged on the sofa, which is pockmarked by cigarette burns, as they pass two joints around between them. Their eyes barely leave the TV set, which is showing an action film, although you wouldn't know it by the viewers' general lethargy. Arranged all around them are materials for making what they are smoking, while empty beer cans are scattered haphazardly across the floor.

'You want a quarter?' John asks.

'Yeh.'

'Got money?'

'Yeh.' Jason looks to Johnny, who fumbles around in his pockets to pull out the money, nearly dropping it on the floor before handing it over. The black guy comes back over to collect it before he and John go into the kitchen.

'Am I all right to smoke in here?' says Johnny to no one in particular, cautiously lighting a cigarette when his question provokes no response. Jason sees his hands are shaking and hopes they can get out of here as fast as possible. His heart is beating like mad, but everything seems to be going well. Good job. John could take their money and tell them to fuck off and they wouldn't be able to do a thing. After what seems like an age the pair reappear from the kitchen and the black guy hands Jason a silver foil package. It is much smaller than he was expecting, but again, there is nothing he can say.

'We'd better be off,' says Jason, warily eyeing the bull mastiff as it appears in the kitchen doorway again.

'You're Denise's brother aren't you?' says John, lighting up a cigarette and leaning against the doorframe.

'That's right.'

'Nice girl, your sister. She was here last night, we had a bit of a party.'

'Oh right,' says Jason, wondering what to say to get them out of the flat. 'She never said.'

'She was totally out of her head. Fucked up my bathroom. Puked all over the place,' says John, emphasising his point with his hands.

'Oh.'

'I need someone to clean it up. I was thinking you two could do it, seeing how it was your sister and everything.' Jason has no idea what to say. Is he serious? He looks it. He sounds it.

'I've got to get back, that's the only thing,' he says.

'That can wait,' says John, his voice turning nasty, his expression closing into a frown. 'I want you to go into my bathroom and clean up the fucking mess your sister made.' Jason looks at Johnny, who looks back at Jason, who looks back at John. 'Now!' John suddenly shouts and they both jump into action, Jason looking to his left where he thinks the bathroom probably is. He hurries over, his heart and stomach doing back flips, with Johnny right behind him. He fumbles with the bathroom door, finally opens it and looks inside. It's already clean. There's nothing to suggest anything untoward has happened in there. Jason's head reels as he tries to work out what to do before he hears laughing from the other room.

'I'm only kidding you dozy bastards,' John manages to say, nearly choking with laughter as though it's the funniest trick anyone has ever pulled.

'I had to clean it myself this morning after she legged it. Ran out of here like a bat out of hell. I thought she was at least going to sort out some breakfast for everyone.' Jason is shell-shocked and doesn't know what to say. He feels as though his whole life has just flashed before his eyes.

'You boys want anything else, anything a bit stronger?'

'No thanks,' says Jason, trying to get his breathing back to normal again.

'Well let me know if you do.'

'Will do,' says Jason. 'See you later.'

'See you later. And Jason?'

'Yeh?'

'You want to calm down mate. You'll have a heart attack one of these days if you're not careful.'

Denise stands in a shop doorway down the road from her house as Dan fumbles around under her fleece. She feels numb but invites his hand all the same, not thinking about last night anymore, but this night and the next night, trying to keep her mind off the fact that come Monday morning she'll be back at Tesco's: every single working day sitting at a till, with Dan the only bit of fun she has. She keeps her eye on the front door of the Labour club, waiting for her dad to go in, then she knows the coast will be clear. Her mum's at the bingo and God knows where her brothers are but they probably won't be back until late so they'll have the house to themselves for an hour or two. They can't go to Dan's place as his dad will be in. For once they'll have a bed to do it in, not like most of the time when they have to make do in alleyways or churchyards or wherever else no prying eyes will see them. Then she spots her dad wandering slowly up to the brick building, wearing one of his better shirts and brown trousers. He's even had a shave. The minute he is out of sight she pulls Dan's hand from under her top and holds it as they cross the road, him ahead of her now, pulling her along, eager to get inside.

She lies back on her bed and closes her eyes as Dan moves around on top of her. She arches her back when he thrusts a bit too hard, but doesn't want to stop him even though she is still feeling sore.

He's not mentioned what happened at the party and she doesn't think he knows, but she doesn't care if she is pregnant anymore. If she is, Dan will take care of her – he's said so before. He's said he'll get her a ring as soon as he's saved up the money. She's already seen one she likes. She opens her eyes for a moment to look at him as he fervently sucks on her neck. She's only just got rid of the last mark, and it's always hell to hide them from her mum, but so what? The weekend is too precious to spend it worrying and so she puts her arms around his neck, pulling him close, wanting his brand on her.

She's had a few boyfriends before but nothing as serious as this. She fancied him the moment she saw him, working in Next in town. She wasn't out looking for anything in particular and saw him serving someone through the window. So she went in, not meaning for anything to happen, not thinking she would say anything. He came over to ask if he could help her, she just said no, but he was stuck in her head from that moment on. And then he was out one Friday night, standing with a group of other lads in The Vic, talking by the bar. She'd told all her mates about him and Vicky went over to him to see if he fancied her. Denise tried to stop her, but inside she wanted her to say something as she didn't have the guts to do it herself. He had looked up when Vicky finished talking and smiled over at her. He was leaving the pub but asked where they were going later. It turned out they were all going to Prince's and so they met on the dance floor, getting off with each other before they'd even spoken a word.

He lives in Pemberton and so they saw loads of each other after that first night, always meeting up with a group of mates and a few bottles of cider. It amazed her how instant the connection had been, that everything fell into place so quickly for them, but it had, and they were still going strong now. She's never been like this before, never wanted a proper boyfriend, happy instead with her mates and whoever came along by chance. At school she'd hung round with one of the hardest girls in her year and so the boys had always found her. They'd go behind the buildings for a smoke and the lads would swarm around them like flies, trying to lift up their skirts or snap their bra straps. She fancied a few of them and went with them one by one, like all the girls did. No one could ever have the front to call her a slag though as she never shagged any of them. She let them do things to her, finger her, feel her up, and she would wank a few of them off every now and then, but she never went all the way with any of them. The closest she came to losing her virginity was when Darren Forshaw spunked all over her school skirt after a heated exchange behind the sports hall. Even then she was free from gaining a tag as she told all her mates about how he'd started even before she touched him, she just pulled him out of his trousers and off he went. The poor lad was laughed at nearly every minute from that day forth. She felt bad about it at first because he was the only one of them she'd even liked, but over time her feelings turned to disgust and thinking he was sad simply because that's what everyone else thought.

Not that she was ever the type to just follow the crowd. When all her mates had their noses pierced she wouldn't, and when they all started taking pills she would turn them down. She pretended to take them, but always managed to get rid of them some other way without actually having to swallow one. And when they all started getting married, straight out of school as well, did she follow them? Like bollocks she did. She hardly sees half of her old mates these days unless they're out round town pushing prams as most of them are up to their eyeballs in kids.

And then there was Claire Green. She was pregnant while they were at school and they had to create a sort of crèche for her when she took her exams because her boyfriend couldn't look after the kid as he was a mechanic and worked through the day. Mind you, she has changed her views on marriage and kids since meeting Dan and because of the women she works with, in their forties and fifties some of them and they still go out on the town looking for men as they're either divorced or have never been married. She does worry about that sometimes, not wanting to end up the way many of them do, either alone and lonely or alone and desperate. Like that time they went out round Wigan, all of them from work together. It was embarrassing, the show Grace made of herself on the dance floor, doing a strip tease to Tom Jones, whirling her top around her head in front of some lad who looked all of eighteen. He didn't know which way to turn and although he laughed while she did it, he looked more relieved than anything when the bouncer finally took her away.

No, I'll never let that happen to me. I will marry Dan, but I'll have a life afterwards. I don't care what my mum says, I'll go to the Tech and do a course in hairdressing. I'll work in a salon washing people's hair and sweeping up and soon I'll get qualified and become a proper hairdresser. Who knows, maybe I'll get my own shop, in an arcade with pictures of people's hair that I've cut, and my name above the window: *Denise's Hair Place*, or *Cut and*

Go. And I won't be like some women, like that Kelly Richards who went with another bloke on a Friday night not three weeks after she was married. She'd only just got back from her honeymoon and I saw her in the pub being pushed against one of the walls, her hands all over him, her leg lifted up against the side of the fruit machine. We'll get married at St Matthews and have a couple of kids. He'll be the manager of Next and I'll run my own shop. We won't just have to go to Blackpool or Morecambe for our holidays, we'll be able to go to Spain, Benidorm, Ibiza, Majorca, Gran Canaria, somewhere hot where you can drink cocktails on the beach and go topless without a load of old pervs staring at you.

She hasn't told Dan that there are plans for her and a few of the girls to go to Ibiza this summer. She doesn't know how he'll react as they are supposed to be going on holiday together themselves. He went to Magaluf with his mates last year, but they'd only just met at the time so there wasn't a lot she could do about it. It's not her fault though, this Ibiza trip, she's been roped into it by her mates at work. They're all ditching their blokes to go away and they don't see why she can't leave Dan for a week. After all, she's not married yet and there'll be plenty of chances for them to go away together in the future, when they've got more money and have been together a bit longer.

Denise grips Dan's back harder as he makes it obvious he's about to come. He's not wearing anything and she's not on the pill anymore but at the moment she has to take her chances, especially after last night. If she was pregnant and they hadn't done it like this then how could she explain that one? He didn't say anything, he never does. She always has to tell him to put a johnny on, he never thinks of it by himself. She went on the pill when she was fourteen as it made her periods regular and not hurt so much. She's always been skinny and back then she was even worse, on the verge of being anaemic at one point. But she had to come off the pill as it made her sick and so it's up to her to remind Dan that he needs something on to be safe. Of course he doesn't like it, no bloke does, but she's not ready to get pregnant just yet, she's got her career to think about. This time she has to let it go though, just in case.

'Have you finished?' she says when Dan finally stops moving and falls onto her chest, sweating.

'Yeh. Have you?'

'Yeh.' She's happy to lie for him, happy to do anything for him.

'Shall we go for a drink?'

'We've got the house to ourselves for the first time in ages. Let's just lie here for a bit. Hold me.'

'What's your Jason up to tonight, has he gone that party?'

'How the fuck should I know?'

'It's just I put him onto Tariq for some gear. I was wondering how he got on.'

'Tariq's nice,' she says, in the way she often does, with a smile on her face to wind him up. His head's on her shoulder so he can't see but she does it anyway.

'Go out with him then,' he says.

'Piss off, you know I only want you,' she says, but knows enough of a seed is there to keep him on his toes. 'What was that noise?'

'Just my stomach I think, I'm starving.'

'No it wasn't, it's the fucking front door! Quick, get up, my parents can't find you in here, they'll kill me.'

Dan jumps out of the bed and starts moving around, desperately trying to find his clothes. The front door slams shut and although she's panicking a bit by this point, she manages a laugh as he fumbles about with his jeans. She watches his dick as it dangles about all over the place, flopping here and there as he pulls his boxers and then his jeans on.

'Hurry up,' she says.

'I'm hurrying.'

Noises come from downstairs and her mum calls out to find out if anyone is home.

'There's only me Mum,' Denise shouts, then whispers to Dan. 'You'll have to go out the window.'

'I know, I've done it enough times by now. I'll probably break my fucking neck one of these days,' he says, opening the window and looking at the drop outside. There's a decrepit caravan in the back yard and he has to lower himself onto it before jumping to the ground and making his way back through the front yard. It's risky but he's never been caught yet.

'Give me a kiss,' she says, leaning over, half her naked body showing from under the sheets. He looks her up and down before kissing her.

'Where shall I meet you after?'

'I can't come out now, not now me mum's back.'

'I'll see you tomorrow then.'

'All right. I love you.'

'I love you too,' he says and is gone. She hears the faint bang as he lands on the roof of the caravan and then onto the back yard. She listens until his footsteps disappear before turning over onto her back. When he's gone it's like he was never there. She looks around the room, but nothing remains. She gets out of bed and puts her dressing gown on before heading downstairs to see if her mum got lucky tonight.

Alexandra Park is only a short walk from Enfield Street, less than half a mile towards town. Like most parks, it looks at its best when the sun is shining, when the trees become elegant shadow-makers and the grass flows like a felt carpet and the flowers by the monument spread their colours across the grey flagged path. The scent of nature is at its headiest after rain has soaked the stems and ground, and in the full light of early afternoon the effect is even more powerful. Mothers push their prams along winding paths that make black trails through the greenery, young lads bring footballs out and play games between jumpers or the metal goal posts with light brown dirt patches underneath where thousands of feet have trampled the grass into dust. The elderly make their way tentatively around the monument to the far left of the park, through the trees which divide the small circular garden from the expanse of green on the other side. Next to the trees two tennis courts remain from the original four, the remainder of the cracked concrete showing a sign of the times after being transformed into a skateboard arena and a basketball court. At the far right there is a sand pit where children play on the rope swing, while picnic benches are occupied by couples or tramps sunning themselves. And overlooking all of this is the embankment holding the train line running from Wigan to Liverpool, tall and imposing, with wild yellow grass haphazardly covering its surface.

Then, as the sun begins to set and the view is hazed by red, the adolescents arrive with their bottles and cans and unrequited sexual tension. As night falls and the park is dimly and sporadically illuminated by passing cars and streetlamps lining the road, the tension drops as alcohol kicks in and furtive passions are quelled. Mesnes Park in town may be larger and more aesthetically pleasing, with its bandstand and duck pond and crazy golf and flower gardens, but at night it takes on a menacing air. Shadows in Mesnes Park could hide a mugger, a rapist, an old drunk with piss in his trousers, but in the darkness of Alexandra teenage lust lies entwined with sticky fingers and underwear down to ankles.

Mark sits dizzily on the swing while moans come from the bushes behind him in quick, quiet bursts. In truth he is hanging on to the plastic-covered chain for dear life even though his feet are barely an inch above the sand beneath him. All the others have long since been paired up and he looks drunkenly at the glinting bottle he dropped what could have been hours ago, his sense of time disappeared almost as soon as he started drinking.

It's always the same ritual. The girls bring bottles of Thunderbird and Concorde, the boys Strongbow or Olde English or Merrydown. Sometimes it's beer, but usually it's cider, he's experienced enough to know that it gets you drunker quicker and for less money. Never sweet cider either, always dry, because it tastes better and it's stronger, although now he wishes he hadn't had quite so much. He's already been sick, twice, but he washed away the taste from the bottle at his feet. A while ago he'd gone over to the bushes to see if he could get a glimpse of what was going on, maybe even join in, but to no avail. Those who were already occupied were happy with their coupling and were anxious to continue their business in peace.

When he looks up there is a lone girl sitting on the edge of the miniature wooden pier leading into the sand. She is staring at him, every now and then swigging from the bottle in her hand. He saw her before, she had the exact wrong shade of ginger hair and too many freckles all over her face and neck to be attractive. Her clothes were about a size too small and made the flab on her drink-expanded young hips slop out over the sides of her jeans. Mark thought she had gone home ages ago.

But she is still there, looking at him over the bottle, swinging her legs over the edge of the pier. In the dark her hair has taken on a brown colour and her freckles have all but vanished in the deep blue glow surrounding them. The petrol station behind the bushes casts the sand pit with more light than other areas of the park enjoy and in this half-light she takes on a new, sexual edge. Mark grips onto the swing and considers the situation for a moment. Why is she looking at him? Is it meant to be provocative, a come-on, a motion for him to go over and have her? He even sobers up slightly as he stares back at her and they sit in silence, looking at each other. Eventually she takes another long drink from the bottle, sighs and looks towards the road.

'Can I have some of your beer?' he says, slurring his words uncontrollably. He hasn't spoken for some time and his voice sounds strange in the semi-silence that is only infrequently disturbed by a car passing by in the near distance or a rustle of leaves behind him.

'Maybe.'

It is all the prompting he needs and he steps uncertainly from the swing across the sand to her, stumbling over the bottle on the floor.

'You're pissed,' she tells him.

'No more than you.'

He drops onto the pier next to her and she hands him the bottle. It is nearly half full still and he takes a tentative swig before handing it back. She is looking at him when she accepts the bottle and he instantly moves in for the kill, tilting his head, mouth half open, hand reaching for her shoulder. She grabs him back with an intensity he hadn't been expecting and was barely ready for. His head reels as she thrusts her tongue into his mouth and he has to stop himself from gagging before he settles into a rhythm. He hears her put the bottle down next to her and he pushes himself round before bearing her back down onto the wooden slats. Then his hand is in action, up her top, making his way over her fleshy stomach and over her bra. He pushes the material aside and flexes his fingers underneath to reach her nipple. After a bit of movement it is erect and when she moans so is he. He didn't think it would be possible in his state and he delights in the possibilities it offers. His hand finishes with her breast after a slight squeeze and begins to make progress back down her body towards her jeans. After a bit of effort he manages to undo the top two buttons when her hand suddenly reaches down to stop him.

'What?' he says.

'I'm not like that.' She pulls his hand away and puts it on her hip.

He is disappointed but not overly so, her mouth is still eager and her hands are strongly grabbing at his back. He puts his hand back under her top and explores her chest again, both sides this time. When her hand strays down to his jeans and starts pulling at the buttons, he knows he won't be rejected again. This time she lifts her arse up so he can pull the jeans over her legs, which takes some effort to complete. Then she does the same to him, grabbing him with her hand and starting to yank. He thrusts his fingers into her, loving how warm and wet it is, and she pulls her mouth away at last to moan out loud. He has to slow down for a minute as her hand is working away on him furiously and he nearly cries in pain as she pulls down extra hard. He keeps his pain unspoken and instead moves so he is on top of her. She looks surprised at first, but he can tell she is willing and he draws himself towards her. Suddenly her hand is there again, stopping his progress, halting his defining moment.

'We can't,' she says.

'Why not?'

'Because we can't.'

'Course we can,' he says. 'There's nothing to stop us.'

'But we're out in the open,' she says, which gives him a glimmer of hope.

'Let's go over there then.' He doesn't wait for an answer, just gets up from the pier and pulls up his trousers.

He looks down and sees her bush in the moonlight. It is much hairier than he thought it would be. Nearly all the naked women he has ever seen, in magazines and films and on television, have not had much hair, just a sliver up the middle. He suddenly becomes very aware of what he is doing, where he is and who he is with. He never imagined losing it like this, in the dark, with a girl he barely knows, having to persuade her that it is a good idea. He always thought the girl would be more than willing, egging him on, talking dirty, that she would be slim and attractive, hopefully quite a bit older, with a glint in her eye that would make him know she wanted him. Then he looks at the girl on the pier, pulling her jeans up just above her waist, not bothering to button them up, not even bothered about kissing anymore. He never thought he would be this drunk, always believing he would be able to remember every moment, savouring the experience and reliving it time and time again in his head. He takes her hand though and pulls her towards the bushes, his heart going like the clappers at the thought of it. He's back to not caring now, it doesn't matter how it happens or who with, as long as it gets done, as long as he can forever be free from the virginal curse.

Then they're at the bushes and he drops his jeans again. She goes at him with the same fervour as before, she's got a better grip this time but her enthusiasm means his groin takes a terrible pounding. He pulls at her jeans and starts kissing her again to try and stop her, pushing her down onto the cold concrete steps between the bushes. He couldn't care less if anyone saw them now, he just wants it over with. Besides, no one is likely to be walking along the path at the top of the steps at this time of night anyway.

He pushes himself onto her, opening her legs with one of his own, and puts his hand down to get his bearings. He is getting a bit nervous now and gives himself a quick rub to get totally in the mood. This is it. This is the moment.

'I don't know about this,' she says.

'Don't be daft.'

'Fuck me!' cries a girl's voice behind them. 'Georgie, what the fuck are you doing here?' The girl throws Mark off her and frantically pulls her jeans back up.

'Where have you been Nic?' she asks. Mark recognises the other girl from earlier in the night.

'Were you two just about to …?' She starts laughing.

Mark looks down at himself, exposed there on the cold steps, and tries to move to cover up, but he gets into a tangled mess and falls over onto his side.

'Come on Georgie, let's go,' the girl says, grabbing her friend and running into the darkness of the park. Mark can hear their hysterical laughter fade into the night as he lies there, his groin feeling bruised. He looks out over the park and can just make out their silhouettes heading across the grass. He doesn't know whether to feel ashamed, cheated by bad luck, or saved from a big mistake, and after pulling his jeans up again he starts to stagger home.

Mark is in the front room, reading a book, *Lord of the Flies*. It's been set for him at school, but for once he likes reading it. Usually he just flicks his way through the texts they give him, hoping to get into them at some point, wanting to learn, but always feeling like he's been given the wrong thing and having to provide his own literary education from the library. Not this time though. He sits in the armchair next to the window and reads, not even thinking about last night anymore, but about Ralph and Piggy and the island. He feels sorry for Piggy, for the way he is treated by the other boys. He empathises with Piggy's desire, and ultimate inability, to fit in, to be accepted, and feels ashamed, for he knows he would be exactly the same if he was like Ralph, tanned and popular. Mark is not fat, but bullies don't just need aesthetic imperfections to use against you.

'Where's your brother?' says his mum.

'Still in bed I think,' says Mark, his eyes never straying from the book in his hands until he hears her yell, 'Jason! Jason! Get out of bed you lazy get, it's nearly two o'clock!'

'Mum, I'm trying to read.'

'Well maybe you should find something more useful to do with yourself.'

Mark wants to say something in reply to this, but knows he'll probably only get a crack if he does. He's pretty sure that reading is useful. He would have thought his mum would appreciate someone in the family trying to get somewhere, trying to get educated and a decent job. Jason left school with five GCSEs and works in whatever factory he can stand for a week or so. Denise got four and works in Tesco's. He wants to get all nine and go to college, maybe even university if he can get funding. He watched a programme the other night about some girl from the North who'd gone to Oxford to study. He saw the streets in the programme, the ancient buildings, the tradition, the pubs that weren't just a big room full of old men getting plastered, but were glorious old buildings where writers and professors had drunk together, talking over intellectual themes beneath the deep wooden beams. That is what he calls useful, but it's not like his mum ever thinks so. She probably wants him to go out and get a job or something. He knows some people whose mothers are proud that they're clever, that they get good grades, that they want to advance themselves. Some kids are encouraged and praised. Anyone who came to his house would think being educated was a character flaw.

'All reet our Mark,' says Denise, coming down the stairs.

'Denise, have you seen your brother?'

'He's still in bed, he was probably on the pop again last night.'

'I'll bloody kill him, he knows we have dinner early on a Sunday. And where the bloody hell's your father?'

'I would hazard a guess that he's down the Labour club,' says

Jason, looking down at them bleary-eyed from the top of the stairs, wearing only jeans and scratching his head.

'And what time d'you call this?'

'I don't know, what time is it?' says Jason, heading for the bathroom.

'Denise, when Jason's finally got himself dressed, you and your brothers go down that bloody Labour club and tell your dad he wants to get himself home before I give his dinner to the dog.'

'Mum we haven't even got a dog.'

'Don't be cheeky, you.'

'Do we really have to go and get him?'

'Aye, shame the bugger into coming home,' she says, going back into the kitchen and muttering under her breath.

'But Mum …,' says Denise, following her.

How the hell he's supposed to get any work done round here is beyond him. It's like a bloody madhouse sometimes. And he can't even have any peace when they're all off somewhere else, there's always something that needs doing. This time it's down to the Labour club to pick up his dad. At least his dad's got somewhere to go to get away from it, not like him. If he sets foot out of the door his mum wants to know where he's going, who with, what time he'll be back. Anyone'd think he was still a kid or something the way he gets treated.

Snooker balls clack together in the saloon bar. The volume on the telly is turned down for now, waiting for the match to start: Wigan against Saints. Frank is as excited as the others about the possibility of a win at Knowsley Road. Men talk and drink and laugh. No one dares to think that tomorrow is Monday. It's too far away to care about for now.

'Ey up Frank, looks like you're wanted at home,' says Albert from behind the bar. 'Lil's sent the kids to fetch you.'

She's done it before, and it's supposed to embarrass him into coming home early. No such luck today, he's here to watch the game and he'll bloody well watch it, just see if he doesn't.

'What you drinking lad?' he says as Jason approaches. He

wasn't expecting that, and neither will she be. 'Pint of John Smith's it is, and a vodka and orange for Denise. Half a Coke Mark? Don't be daft, have a pint.'

'But Mum's wanting you back for dinner.'

'Don't you worry about her lad. Have you met my kids, Bert? What's she moaning for anyway, doesn't she know Wigan are playing today? Here, have a drink and after you've had that, have another, she'll come over soon enough.'

'What about dinner?'

'If you're hungry lad, have something here. Pork scratchings, Bert. Do you want some crisps Denise? Here Jason, take this money and get the drinks in, I'm off to the gents.'

'Mum'll kill him,' says Mark.

'Stop worrying,' Jason tells him. 'It's nothing to do with us if she does.'

'It's full of dirty old men in here, I feel like I'm being watched.'

'Who'd watch you? Here, get this down your neck and stop moaning, you're as bad as mum sometimes.'

'And you're as bad as our dad. I don't know why you're drinking anyway, you must have had enough last night.'

'It's the weekend isn't it? I can have a drink if I feel like it. God knows you need a drink when you can get one.'

'I've got work tomorrow.'

'All the more reason to have a drink now, it'll be next Friday before you get another one.'

'Mum won't be happy about this,' Mark mutters.

'She won't notice,' Jason says. 'I saw her heading over the road when we were leaving, she'll be bending Jean's ear for a bit yet.'

well my Frank was telling me that sooner or later they're going to be laying people off at Heinz's what with the recession and everything but he's not worried he reckons it's just a scare tactic to get some of the managers to leave early but it's like that everywhere these days no one's safe in their job not like the old days when you had a job for life I mean my dad worked on the buses all his life there's none of that now though no certainty in anything apart from that another day'll follow this one and maybe the money will keep coming in it's like our Denise at Tesco's she's nearly been there a year and you'd think that'd count for something but I'll tell you what it doesn't it makes no difference at all anymore mind you she says she might want to become a hairdresser in the future I told her that there's more chance of management at Tesco's or moving up to the offices but she won't listen well they never do she thinks she knows best I'll tell you I wish I'd had someone around to tell me what to do when I was seventeen but the only encouragement you ever got back then was a clip round the ear and get on with it you couldn't get away with that sort of thing these days at least she's got a boyfriend now though he's got a good job she's been with him a fair while too although I'm not expecting wedding bells just yet and I've told her she's got to be careful he might be a nice lad and everything but the rate girls her age are getting knocked up it's frightening they think it's all the rage having a baby they don't know the half of it I blame these bloody celebrities I mean I was only young when I had Jason not that I regret it like but you do wonder what could have happened if it hadn't happened so early I worry about our Mark he's always got his head stuck in some book or other I worry that he's becoming a bit soft I wish he'd settle down and go out and get a job or something but he's a dreamer that lad always has been since he was a little 'un always had his head in the clouds he's on about going to college or university but who's got the money for that sort of thing on my wage from the Hospice and our Frank at Heinz I don't bloody think so but he won't listen none of them will but they're not as bad as some of the kids you read about there's no respect anymore not like when we were young you had to look up to your elders and earn your own keep then as soon as you could there was no help coming from anywhere else they get away with murder these days some people I was telling Doris at the bingo last night it's a bloody cheek I said to her I told her what I thought about it and no mistake him next door claiming on the disability for nearly two years and not a care in the world and going on two holidays last year it's a load of nonsense if you ask me not that any of them ever would the ignorant so and so's they think they know it all some people but I'm wise to their ways they're common that's the only word for it common as muck with kids looking like they've never had new clothes for I don't even know how long and him walking about in the garden in his be all it's a bloody sight I don't want to look at when I'm having a cup of tea in the afternoon or any other time for that matter I mean my Frank may not have a lot but at least he's not a skiver because that's what he is and I don't care if he knows that's what I think of him I'd say it to his face if I had half a chance and then there's that little scrubber daughter of theirs pregnant again and she's not even nineteen it's a scandal what goes on and there's no father in sight like we need another bastard around here it'll probably turn out half-caste if I know anything about it I've seen her hanging around the estates with that Asian lad from the Post Office I can't understand how he's turned out the way he has when his father's such a nice bloke all gold jewellery and fast noisy cars that fog up the place I'd send 'em bloody home the lot of 'em if it was up to me causing trouble and making it so you can't walk down the street at night and feel safe I'll tell you one thing for certain our Jason would never have nothing to do with his sort he may not be an angel or anything but I know he's not into drugs or anything like that he likes a drink a bit too much sometimes but at the end of the day he's a good lad he's just got another job you know down at that carpet factory just outside town it's good money too and no night shifts like that other place where he was chopping up melons for hours on end or whatever it was oh he didn't like that well who would coming home at all hours and having no life outside of work well you can't carry on like that he's only young still he wants to at least try and enjoy himself God knows he'll have to work for long enough so he might as well find something he wants to do I told him to pack that one in even before they sacked him which they only did because he didn't want to put up with the circumstances he was in not like that bloody layabout next door who wouldn't know what a job was if it came up and bit him he says he's got a dodgy back but I've seen him messing about in that garden forever messing about with his plants and buggering up my fence

The main room is red: red lights, red walls, red chairs, red. They're all sitting at a table on the raised part near the back, the best place to see the stage. The club is getting full now, people drifting in for a bit of an escape, full from Sunday dinners, bored of the telly and wanting a drink. The rows of long tables leading from the stage to the raised area are almost all full, while old couples sit in the lounge room out back and the rest of the men play snooker or watch telly in the saloon bar. Wigan have won and Frank is boisterous. Lil may not have got the numbers in the bingo game that afternoon, but the drink sees to it that she doesn't care. Jason's got talking to a girl he used to go to school with over by the bar, Dan has his arm around Denise, and Mark is talking loudly as the pints catch up on him and his enthusiasm is finally engaged. Tonight's turn is about to come on stage and the lights dim as laughter rings out from the table. Empty glasses clutter the table before Bert's son comes round to collect them, Mark smiling that it isn't him tonight, enjoying being on the other side, the drinker's side, for once.

They've all been down there for hours but no one has any intention of leaving. Even Lil's bad mood at dinner being put on hold has dissipated now, forgotten forever after having gone down the chippy. Frank plied her with drinks the minute she walked in, the scowl on her face felt by everyone, especially Jason, Denise and Mark, who hid behind their father until he had calmed the situation down. She'd wanted to see the game anyway and when all eyes focused on the telly in the corner, the snooker table abandoned for the first time that day, she had cheered with the rest of them when the tries started to flow, had held onto Frank's arm when St Helens staged a late comeback, and leaned on the bar with relief when the hooter went at full time, ordering drinks for everyone herself. Mark was delighted to be involved, he thought he would be the first one to cop it, especially given the look on his mum's face when she saw the half empty pint glass in his hand. But Frank had been on good form, calming her down, giving her a cuddle and buying the beers. She'd forgotten the row in her head not ten minutes after she'd walked in, and now her cheeks were red with merriment and her head dizzy with ale.

The turn comes onto the stage, a young bloke with a frilly white shirt and tight leather trousers. Lil is taken in immediately, eyeing him up and down, laughing with Denise at the all too evident bulge, giving out a wolf whistle before he even starts singing. He goes into a few of the old classics, numbers by the Four Tops and Tom Jones. Lil remembers the time she saw The Beatles at the Ritz in town, how not a soul in the place had heard any music because the screaming was so loud. The building had been turned into a cinema which had since been closed down, but the memory always brings a smile to her face whenever she goes to the bingo next door. Those days might be long gone, but she can still see herself as she was then, all bleached-blonde hair and mini-skirted up. Not much has changed really, except maybe the skirts on the girls in town are even shorter these days. She remembers the look on Frank's face when he first laid eyes on her. He looked as though his tongue was set to drop out of his head. She'd walked into the club that night and he'd bought her drinks from the off. He might be a bit fuller round the gut these days, but the drinking and the good times were still there when he put his mind to it.

'Look at that fool, who does he think he is with them trousers and that shirt? All he needs now is a bloody medallion.'

'Oh shut up Dan, you'd not think anything of it if that was a young girl with her tits hanging out.'

'Leave off Denise, the lad's right – if that bloke's face was any oranger he'd be radioactive.'

'I think he's got a good voice. Reminds me of Billy Fury.'

'Billy bloody Fury? Are you deaf woman?'

'Who's Billy Fury, Dad?'

'Someone who sounds bugger all like that clown up there.'

'He's doing his best Frank, and Denise is right, you wouldn't think twice if that were a Judith Durham look-alike.'

'I don't know about you Dan, but I'm off in the other room for a bit of peace. Come on Mark.'

'Leave him here, he's all right with us.'

'Suit yourself.'

Mark is aware of what is going on, but only in the vaguest sense of the word. He doesn't mind though, he feels grown up going out drinking with his family. Jason and Dan often go out with his dad, but his mum very rarely lets him go along too, so this is a special occasion for him. He doesn't think he wants to move, he feels quite sure if he stood up he'd be sick. He can just about see the man on the stage, but it's like when he looked through someone's glasses at school, everything is cock-eyed and out of focus. He can hear him singing well enough though, and looks to see the smile on his mum's face as she watches and sways along with the music. Denise's eyes flick from the stage to the door that Dan and his dad have just left through, but she puts her hand to her mouth and laughs with her mum when the singer starts wiggling his hips around for effect, realising most of his audience is now female.

Denise is thinking that the singer looks like a stripper she once saw on a hen night. He'd been fucking gorgeous, all muscles with a smooth, tanned chest. She and Michelle had gone into the pub's back room where he was changing afterwards because he'd made eyes at both of them. He'd given them a private show then and there, but this time taking off the skimpy G-string he'd worn when he'd made Jane lick cream off his stomach. Denise had never seen anything like it when he took everything off, the biggest cock she'd ever seen in her life. It must have been half way down his thigh and swung about like a pendulum when he moved his hips. She sometimes puts herself back in that room, without Michelle, wondering what she would have said and done if it had just been the two of them. What she wouldn't have done to have that thing inside her. As it was, she and Michelle had just screamed and run back to the pub, telling all the other girls about it. But when they tried to see him again the door to the room had been locked and they'd gone on to the next pub instead.

'Do you want another drink Mum?'

'No thanks love, I'm all right. Here, take this fiver, get yourself and Mark another one though.'

Jason cannot believe his luck. He's hardly bought a drink all day, he's managed to get pissed, and who should walk in near the end of the rugby but Nicola fucking Allbright, the girl he fancied all the way through school. Even though he got on well with her and often saw her about on nights out, he'd never managed to get anywhere near. There was one time when she'd asked him for a birthday kiss, but that had just been a brief touch of lips, nothing more. For about two years she'd been his wanking material, and he'd use the thought of her and what he wanted to do to her when he didn't have a magazine handy. Now she was standing right in front of him and had been talking to him for over an hour, ditching her brother after walking in and turning her attention to him. She'd been one of the fittest girls in his year, everyone wanted to get near her, but that honour was mainly reserved for older lads. She could be friends with lads her own age, but it was definitely not the done thing to go out with them, and besides, the older lads who wanted to make a move on her would make sure no one else had a chance. But that was a long time ago and Jason was going to make sure he didn't let this golden opportunity pass him by. The crunch moment comes when she has to leave, her brother wanting to get home because he's at work in the morning. And for once he doesn't let it go. When the awkward moment comes and she's about to follow her brother out the door, Jason grabs her arm and stops her, asks her for her phone number. They spend a minute with mobiles at the bar swapping numbers, saying they'll text each other in the week and then she finally is gone, but it doesn't matter. After missing out before he always thought it was his destiny never to get with her, never to have a chance at turning fantasy into reality. He wonders if he has some new-found courage that he wasn't aware of, or if it's just the drink helping him talk, but whatever it is, the end result is the same. Her number is in his phone and he'll see her soon. He is so dumbstruck he doesn't even notice when Denise comes up to him at the bar.

'Do you want a drink Jay? What are you grinning for?'

'Nothing.'

'Can't be nothing, you're like a Cheshire cat you are.'

'Probably because it's the weekend, Sis. I'll have another pint if you're buying.'

Working Week

In the factory Jason is fuming. He's got twice as much to do because the fuck-up he was working with has had to go to hospital. They give you these cotton wool things to put in your ears to deaden the noise when you're near the bigger machines and the complete nob has put them so far in they've got stuck. He'll probably need surgery for God's sake. Not that Jason cares what happens to Dave, he just wants to take things easy. As if work wasn't bad enough on its own, he gets stuck with a guy who drones on and on about Canada, how he went out there for a year, how he worked out there, cash in hand, made a fortune – bought a big car and everything. He was going to stay there but things fell through between him and his bird. They were about to get married, he'd bought her a ring and it was all set, but then one day she wasn't there anymore. Literally just upped and left him, no note, no clothes, no car, no nothing. Fuck knows how he found a bird in the first place, thinking about it. But now he's got over it and wants to go back. He looks like a mental patient or something and probably only got this job because the fucking jobcentre couldn't find any other thing the numb bastard could do. And he couldn't even do that right. Jason would smile if he wasn't so pissed off.

He doesn't even want to be here in the first place but his mum put pressure on him to get a job, so he took this one. It's as good as any other and it isn't too hard to get to in the morning: bus into town, then a quick bus out again. He has to start at seven thirty in the morning but he's finished by four. He has no intention of keeping it up for long. Mind you, if his supervisor has anything to do with it, he'll probably be leaving even sooner. The stuck-up cunt. He's one of those manager types who think they have to wear a moustache to look important. Jason reckons he was in the army before, a sergeant major, and the way he acts you'd think he was still there: going round on his fork lift, barking orders left, right and centre, saying everything Jason's doing isn't up to scratch – 'do it again, do it faster.' Fuck it all. All he has to do is chuck cardboard into a crusher, cardboard boxes, tubes, cones, anything cardboard goes in. The supervisor actually stressed: 'No plastic, just cardboard. Any plastic gets in there and it'll fuck the whole thing up.' As if he can't work out the difference between cardboard and plastic for fuck's sake.

Saying that though, it's better than the last place, the crisp warehouse, where he'd had to work nights and it totally messed his life up. Ten at night until six in the morning, he's never doing that again, that's for certain. It started off okay, he managed to blag his way onto a motorised pallet truck, he'd never driven one before, but it wasn't like you needed to be the brains of Britain to do it. He actually had fun, speeding around the warehouse, picking up loads of boxes and stacking them onto lorries. But then he'd turned up one Friday night and all the trucks had been taken, so they put him working on the packing machine. He had to go and pick up the pallets of crisp boxes with a normal truck, the kind you have to pull around and pump up yourself, and bring them over to this metal thing on the ground that spun round. Attach a bit of cellophane around the bottom, then hold the button down until the whole thing was covered. Then you took the load back and got another one. He did it for about twenty minutes before deciding to pack it in. It was Friday night for fuck's sake and there were a million better things he could be doing with his time.

So he went outside, got his car, and drove to Wigan to get pissed with his mates. He got a phone call the next day telling him not to bother going back, but he didn't care. Nine days on nights had given him enough money to finance his weekend and a few nights after that, but he'd quickly got broke again.

'Hey Shag,' shouts the sergeant major. He calls everyone in the place 'Shag', like it's some big joke or something.

'What?' Jason shouts back.

'Make sure you don't fuck up, I'm going on me dinner.'

Don't fuck up? How could anyone doing this job possibly fuck up? You stand in front of this big crushing machine and throw bits of cardboard into it. Anyone who can get that wrong needs locking up. It wasn't so bad at first, the radio is cranked up nice and loud and he's nowhere near the machines that actually make the carpet. He remembers being taken around Wigan Pier when he was at school, and when you went over the road to Trencherfield Mill they put the machines on for a few minutes to show you how loud it was for the women who worked there. Of course, most of the poor bastards went stone deaf after a few years. It's the same in this place though, the machines are loud as fuck when they're turned on full. Jason does manage a smile this time when he thinks of Dave putting that cotton wool so far in his ears it wouldn't come out. Poor, stupid bastard. They'll probably sack him for that as well. Working with him hadn't been that bad he supposed. It was a damn sight better than when he'd started a couple of weeks ago, when he'd been in a different part of the factory and all he'd had to do was stick these plastic stoppers in the four corners of carpet square after carpet square. Eight hours of that and your brain starts turning to mush. But recently all he's had to do is crush any leftover cardboard, tie up the mangled squares with some plastic and leave them to one side. He even tried livening things up by playing a game, throwing the bits in from different angles, kicking the cones from imaginary free-kick spots.

At the end of the day though, it's just like every other job, boring as shite after a while. Like that melon place, Jesus Christ, you could go insane doing that for any length of time. Mountains of melons coming down a conveyor belt, hacking one after another in half. They'd be in trouble giving a guy like Dave one of the big knives they use in there, he'd probably end up chopping himself in half. Or like when he had to pick off the excess bits from moulded plastic shapes on yet another conveyor belt just so they'd fit into Hoovers or whatever the hell they were meant for. Every time he gets bored or pissed off at what he's doing and he either jacks it in or gets sacked first. Then it's back to the job-centre, where job hunting basically means picking a factory or a warehouse to work in. Yet to get pissed he needs money, and so he goes back again and again, looking for something to do, hoping it'll be bearable. Fun doesn't even enter into it. The only job satisfaction is picking up his pay at the end of the week and spending it. It all seems too far away on a Tuesday afternoon though.

Jason throws another cardboard cone onto the lot already lying in the crusher and goes over to press the green button that'll bring the big metal press down and squash all the bits together. As he keeps his finger on the button, watching the cones getting flattened one by one, he catches sight of the sergeant major's fork lift out of the corner of his eye and gets a great idea.

Tesco's stands where Central Park, the former home of Wigan rugby, used to be. The roads are still pretty much the same as they always were, apart from a new side entrance to get to the supermarket. When Denise walks down the big dual carriageway towards her work she almost feels the way she did when she and her dad would walk down this way to watch the games. There used to be row upon row of red and white down this road, all making their way to the focal point of Wigan, Central Park. But as with most things, even that has changed, another part of her childhood is erased by progress. She shouldn't complain because at least she now has a place to work, but memories are sometimes more valuable than a pay cheque. Her brothers never used to come along as they only liked the football and when her dad was off somewhere watching Latics with them, she'd go down to Central Park with some of her mates from school, ready to drool over Gary Connolly or Henry Paul with shorts right up to their arses, powerful legs pumping like pistons underneath. Now the rugby and football teams play at the same stadium, the JJB, which is all very posh, with a cinema and places like Pizza Hut and Kudos nightclub next door. It's certainly more impressive than Springfield and Central Park put together, but somehow it doesn't feel the same, especially when she walks the route again, now having to face another shift behind a till rather than the prospect of seeing blokes maul each other on a muddy pitch.

Once behind her till, instead of the lines of red and white along the terraces, she sees lines of people pushing trolleys, lines of shelves, huge colourful displays packed with every conceivable item, and the conveyor belt of shopping, each time offering a momentary insight into the lives of those queuing. She has time to think at work, probably the only time she ever really has for her mind to wander and imagine. She does not need to think about what she is doing, her hand moves along mechanically, sweeping the items across the scanner, the beep becoming a monotonous rhythm like a computerised heartbeat, mirroring her own. Packets of cornflakes, cases of beer, boxes of burgers, teabags and fishcakes, washing up liquid, spaghetti and sauce, tins of tuna and corned beef and peaches, tomato sauce, tampons, bottles of milk, potatoes, bin liners, lasagne for one, frozen pies, frozen peas, tins of chopped liver, even bags filled with bananas or apples or onions do not break the routine, her hand placing these items onto the metal weighing machine without having to think about it once. She looks up now and then to repeat the price shown on the screen, accepting cash or coupons or cheques in the same manner, none of it requiring any real thought, she has worked here long enough now to be able to switch onto autopilot for a few hours.

She is late, but she has not told Dan. At the moment there is nothing to tell him. Her periods had always been dead on regular when she had been on the pill, but since she came off it some months are easier to gauge than others. Maybe this is just one of those months. Maybe. She has bought pregnancy testing kits, but thrown them away before using them. She cannot face the thought of it, cannot deal with what a positive result might mean, what will happen to her if she is expecting. When they have talked about it before, safe in hypotheticals, he has said he will stand by her, but she cannot afford to have a baby now whether he will or not. There are other girls she knows who have had kids and their life pretty much ended the moment they left the delivery room. They push prams around, they look tired, they have to go on the social and live in a council flat. If Dan does do right by her then she will not have to do any of that, but she still has too much to achieve before she can think of having a child. She has to go to college. She has to study to become a hairdresser, and then she can start work away from here, away from those who make their way through the supermarket, as through life, like sheep, herded along by things beyond their control simply because they do not choose to alter their destiny. And then there's the holiday she's supposed to be going on. Yet another thing she hasn't mentioned to Dan, and yet another thing that plays on her mind. Any trip to Ibiza will most definitely be out the window if there is a kid growing inside her.

There are other concerns too, far more worrying thoughts that she is slowly trying to consign to the recesses of her mind. It might not even be Dan's, but some unknown person's at the party. She has tried time and time again to think back to what happened, who was there, who she was talking to. But all she can remember is gripping the sides of the toilet bowl, looking into the gathering mess in the water, and then blackness, nothingness. And then there was light. The next day, and her knickers were around her knees and the only notion she has as to what has happened is the soreness between her legs and the dried-up flakes.

She knows there are other ways out. Debbie Gray had it done just after they left school. She'd gone a bit mad in the summer, slept with God knows how many blokes, and the next thing she knew she was up the duff with no way of knowing who the father was. So she'd decided to get rid of it and asked Denise to go with her to the hospital. They'd put her in a bed and given her some pills to flush it out. Denise can remember the way Debbie had bitten her lip almost to bleeding to stop herself from making any noise, contracting time and time again, gripping Denise's hand as her stomach cramped and pushed and cramped again. Debbie didn't stop crying throughout the whole thing, vowing never to sleep with another bloke as long as she lived. Saying it wasn't worth the hassle, it wasn't worth this, none of it. After an hour or so it had come out, dropped into a cardboard bedpan thing. Debbie hadn't wanted to look, besides, she had been throwing up since it had happened and only stopped properly when the nurse had taken the bedpan away.

But Denise had looked. She had been compelled to see what all the fuss was about, what could have caused so much pain. And there it was, an odd shaped crimson ball swimming in a soup of sticky dark blood. She'd somehow been able to stop herself from retching at the sight of it before the nurse came, but the vision of that bloody mess has stayed with her ever since. She'd managed to forget about it for a few hours, they'd gone straight to the pub afterwards to drink away the pain and the memory, Debbie laughing again, the beer making her face flushed once more after having been ghostly white for most of the day. They'd even got talking to some lads and Debbie had gone off with one of them later on, leaving Denise to stumble home on her own.

It kills her to think that she would not say anything to Dan, but what choice does she have? She cannot tell him what she thinks has happened, after all, it may not even matter. But if it does, she has to hide the possible truth. And as she works through the day, her hand swiping items through the scanner, she becomes convinced within her mind that if she is pregnant, it is Dan's, for the thought of anything else is too horrific to comprehend. So she begins to plan for her future as though she is pregnant, imagining herself and Dan bringing up the child together, a little girl, buying it things, going to the park together, her face a mixture of both of theirs, pretty and small and innocent. She will get another pregnancy kit and she will take it this time. She will sit there and watch to see if a line appears, unravelling the route her life must take from then on. Not knowing is far worse, no matter what the outcome eventually is. She passes condoms, three packs, and a packet of mints through the till and this time she looks up to see who is buying.

'All right Denise.'

'Tariq,' she says, her guard down. She has no need for flirtation when Dan is not around. 'What are you doing here?'

'Buying supplies,' he says, and for once Denise sees something else behind his smile, something that bothers her slightly, makes her skin creep. There are people queuing up behind him and looking annoyed that they may have to wait while this girl chatters away.

'I can't really talk,' she says.

'I'll see you around. Maybe later?'

'Yeh, see you,' she says, looking at the woman standing next in line to be served. Her chain of thought is broken, but only for a moment, and the next minute she is back buying baby clothes.

In school the other kids make fun of him. He's not even been back a month and it's already at fever pitch. He likes books, he writes poetry, he is in turns called a 'geek', an 'arse-licker', a 'swot', 'gay' even, and he is harried about as he makes his way into the classroom. As if studying is something to be mocked. He's in his final year for God's sake, just months away from taking GCSEs, his ticket out of this place, away from these people who'd drag him down with them given half a chance. He's going to get away. He has to get away, it doesn't matter where, anywhere has to be better than here. He's been reading Goethe recently and mutters under his breath when they kick him on purpose in games or shout him down in class, his new secret philosophy: *Whatever you can do, or dream you can do, begin it. Boldness has genius, power, and magic in it.* He hopes he can be bold enough, push himself to achieve what he dreams of achieving; go through his life without haste, without rest. He may not be able to do anything ground breaking here, but his motto drives him on, makes him want to listen in class, do his homework on time, be uncool for now if it means reaping the rewards later.

He pays little heed to the name-calling for the most part, but sometimes it is thrust in his face so he cannot ignore it, or is spoken so loudly that even the girls laugh at him. He knows they are scared, that they cannot show weakness for fear that they too will become a target for the verbal battering. Bullying is rife and the subject of it can be altered by one false move, one step in the wrong direction, a single word out of place. He is scared too, but he does not let it show. He is biding his time, waiting to get out, ready to use any means necessary to get to college and university and away from this hole of a high school. He does have friends, but it is the unpleasant episodes that stick so certainly in his mind when he is at home or when he gets a minute alone. He sits reading a book on a bench away from the others, hoping not to be seen in this refuge behind the staff room, but still they find him and the taunting continues, one boy tipping his book out of his hands and onto the floor, much to the delight of his mates.

He is set to get 'A's in his results, that's what all his teachers say. They are the one set of people who do not make fun of him. Even his parents cannot understand his passion for learning. But teachers must be avoided, too much attention and the derision is amplified to soul destroying levels. Of course not everyone is the same, there are others who share his dreams for the future, but they too are hounded down and ridiculed and stay quiet like he does. There is no group mentality for those who want to try, no true places to hide, only varying success rates in avoiding degradation. The mob is strong among the cynical, those who seem to want to underachieve if only to avoid standing out from the crowd.

Then there is the problem of what to do when you need the toilet. Pissing is naturally par for the course, when the boys gather at urinals and pretend they are not sneaking a look at how developed their neighbour is. But going for a shit is something to be ridiculed, where if you are sitting down in a cubicle and someone finds you, they will peer over the top and laugh at you, telling everyone in class what you have just been doing. Sometimes they throw water over at you, and the drenching your head and shoulders receive makes you a marked man, more open than ever to the inevitable taunts. Mark has wondered in the past how the other boys get round this, the ones who are all too quick to take the piss out of you simply because you have to take a dump. He always needs to go to the toilet around dinnertime, but he can't for fear of reprisals. He has found some toilets that are hidden from most prying eyes, away from the usual corridors, up near the science blocks, but more often than not they are locked or unavailable due to vandalism. Now he just accepts that this is the way, that he must hide his need, hold it in, try to wait until he is back home.

However, one day he can't manage to wait, he really needs to go. After searching his usual haunts, each time beginning to relax as he approaches and then having to tense up again when he finds them closed, he stands alone in the alcove near the front yard after games, his bowels pushing hard on him, his stomach cramping unbearably. And so he lets it out, relishing the relief, but uncomfortable in the warmth now resting in his trousers. The bell goes and he shuffles forward towards class, the last of the day, hoping he can keep it in his underpants until he can get home. What he doesn't realise is that the smell is incredible and the minute he lines up to walk into class people are holding their noses and asking, 'Who did it, who farted, who's the dirty bastard?' Mark stands in silence as the accusations fly, the furore only quietening when the teacher arrives and ushers them inside. He sits down and the lesson begins. After only a couple of minutes though, anyone sitting near him has their nose wrinkled in disgust, people looking round and wondering where the stench is coming from. Fear rises in Mark as he realises he will be discovered at any moment and so he quickly stands, hoping the mess in his trousers cannot be seen from behind, telling the teacher he doesn't feel well and running from the room the minute he is through the door.

In the Pagefield they are merry with drink and sun. Outside it glints off car windscreens and white T-shirts, creating a haze along the tarmac of the undulating roads that cross at the pub. Inside the rays pick out trails of blue fog from cigarettes placed on the edge of the pool table, the pockets bunged with beer mats so that no more than thirty pence is needed for an afternoon-long game. Pints are arranged on the tables at the side and Jason lines up another shot as Nicola tries to put him off by pinching his arse. He has never been happier, here with Nicola and Johnny and Craig and Donna and Louise. A month ago he thought he'd probably never see Nicola Allbright again, confined instead to thinking about her from time to time and maybe bumping into her on a Friday night on King Street. But he's been seeing her steadily since that fateful night in the Labour club, at first only meeting her in the company of their friends, feeling their way, until finally being able to go out together, just the two of them. Nothing has been said as to whether or not they are officially 'going out' but in many ways it can happily remain unspoken. They have not slept together yet, which took Jason by surprise. He heard a rumour about her at school that she had wanked someone off in a cinema on their first date, but while she has had her hand on him, wheedling her fingers down the front of his jeans one night in the front of her car, she has made no motions towards having sex.

She has not shagged as many people as he thought she would have. He knows she must have had the opportunities, pretty much every boy at school had wanted her. He would not have dumped her if she had told him she had slept with more, but the idea that she is not a slag makes him feel more about her than anyone he has ever been with in the past. And so he is happy to wait. Usually in this situation he would get rid of her quickly, no action means it goes no further as far as he's concerned. But she is different, when it happens it will be better than ever before, special. The idea he'd have these sort of thoughts would have made him want to throw up before, but not now. For once he feels totally at ease, she's even met his mum when she came round to pick him up one time before they went to the cinema. And for once she fits in with his friends, she is already a part of the group, and it cracks him up no end that he and Johnny get to hang around with the girl they used to spend hours talking about when at school, discussing everything from her figure and her hair to whether she'd ever go with either of them. He smiles as he slides the cue over his bridged fingers and the balls crack together, whirling around the table, and he isn't even surprised that he doesn't care when nothing goes down.

'So what happened to the job then Jay?' asks Craig, taking the cue from Jason's hand.

'They sacked me the other day.'

'You got sacked again?' said Johnny.

'It wasn't my fault this time. The supervisor was a total pain in the arse, he wanted me out the minute I walked in.'

'So what did you do to get sacked?'

'I got the bastard back,' said Jason, drinking from his pint and trying to hide his smirk.

'What did you do?' said Nicola, a feigned tone of disapproval in her voice.

'Well, he was always going round on his fork lift like he was lord of the fucking manor, so when he went to the canteen for his dinner, I just made sure he'd stay on his precious machine when I started winding him up.'

'What did you do?' Nicola repeated, digging him in the ribs.

'When he came back from his dinner, he started shouting at me again, do this, do that, not that way, this way, like he had been all the time I'd been there. So I listened to him and then called him a Nazi dog-loving paedophile with a whore for a wife.'

'You did what?' said Craig, abandoning the shot he'd been lining up. 'What the fuck did he do?'

'There was nothing he could do, I'd put some industrial glue on his fork lift seat, so I just told him to fuck off and walked out while he sat there scrabbling about like a dickhead.'

'You fucking never!' cried Nicola.

'I think that deserves another pint,' said Johnny, grinning as he headed off for the bar.

'What are you going to do now?' said Louise.

'Get pissed,' said Jason.

It's Thursday, only forty-eight hours after he pulled the stunt that had ended his job at the carpet factory, but Jason is already sure the memory of what happened will stay with him for quite some time yet. Almost the minute his supervisor had gone for dinner he'd had the idea. There was a big tube of glue lying near one of the piles of cardboard boxes he was getting ready to crush and once he was sure no one would see what he was doing, he'd made his way over to the abandoned fork lift and sprayed it all over the seat. He hadn't been worried that he'd snare the wrong person, the sergeant major never let anyone other than himself drive the fork lift he used, but he had been slightly afraid that he'd see the white glue spread over the seat. He'd hidden it as well as he could, putting as much as possible over the patches of paint already staining the black plastic, but some of it was still easily visible if you looked. But the sergeant major hadn't looked. He'd just come straight back from the canteen, jumped up into the fork lift and driven over to Jason, who was lazing around on purpose in anticipation. The sergeant major had started in on him straight away, asking him why he was sitting down, why he was smoking when it wasn't allowed in the building, there were piles of cardboard to be crushed, and the piles he'd already done hadn't been done right. Jason just sat there while he was barked at before telling the sergeant major in no uncertain terms to fuck himself. He doesn't remember ever laughing quite as much as he did when he walked out of the factory's side entrance while the sergeant major flailed around helplessly, his face boiling red as he struggled to understand why he suddenly couldn't stand up.

Johnny brought new pints into the back room, sitting them on the mantelpiece over the old fireplace near the pool table. Jason didn't come to the Pagefield that often, only when Craig was out of work and up for a piss up as he now was. The all day sessions they've had there in the past have turned out to be legendary, usually taking them onto King Street and the pubs in town until the early hours of the morning. Craig, Johnny and Jason had all gone to school together and were the only people in their class any of them had kept in touch with thereafter. They often saw people from their year around town, but met up with them out of coincidence rather than arrangement. Craig lived quite close to the pub, in a house near Mesnes Park, and had rung Jason and Johnny on the off-chance they would have the day off like him. He needn't have worried, Johnny was in the middle of a four day off period, he worked in a bottle packing factory doing twelve hour shifts. The work was hard but the pay was worth it and when the days off fell over a weekend, Johnny could even forget about how much he hated working there. Nicola had been at the bank when Jason called and her manager had sent her off with sympathy when she developed a migraine over dinner. Louise, Johnny's bird, didn't work, she lived at home with her mum and her kid and claimed the dole, while Donna, Craig's younger sister, worked the late shift in The Tudor. And so they'd all gathered to spend the day together, to drink and forget about working for a while.

Nearly five o'clock. The beers are starting to tell on them and the endless pool games are getting monotonous. They've had pretty much all the songs they want to hear on the juke box, spending most of their time singing along to The Verve, Oasis, The Beatles, Madness, Starsailor, Stereophonics, dance tunes, anthems, even Frank Sinatra have all been worn out at this point and it is Craig who comes up with the plan.

'There's a way to get into the cellar you know. Me and me brother found it last time we were in here. We were well wrecked and started wandering about. You go down these stairs until you get to a door and there's a key on the wall that opens it and it's the cellar and you can get all the beer you want.'

So they follow Craig while Donna stands at the door and keeps watch. When no one's looking they head down the stairs. Inside it's pitch black and they try hard to keep themselves from talking or laughing too loud. Craig fumbles with the door at the bottom of the stairs and after opening it, switches on a light.

'This isn't a cellar,' says Jason, trying to steady himself against the side of the stairs.

'It's a bloody kitchen,' says Johnny. 'What the fuck are we doing in a kitchen Craig?'

'I must have got the wrong door.'

'Hang on,' says Nicola, 'Check the fridge.'

'Fuckin' 'ell there's a bottle of vodka in here!' cries Johnny, holding the bottle aloft. 'And it's full too.' They are all laughing out loud now, unable to control themselves any longer. Louise looks as though she's about to piss herself. The laughter stops when they hear noises from above. Confusion and silence reign for a moment before Johnny decides what to do, sprinting back up the stairs, the others close behind, pushing the old bloke standing by the door at the top of the stairs out of the way and running from the building, straight towards the park and Craig's house. Jason holds Nicola's hand as they run, laughing as they hear shouting coming from behind them. The others follow Johnny's lead, straight back into Craig's house to drink their prize, but just as Jason is about to follow them over the road, Nicola pulls him towards the park.

'What about the others?' he says.

'The others can wait.'

When her shift ends Denise places the two pregnancy kits she has lifted from the shelves into her bag. She doesn't steal often, and only takes things she needs, but always feels like a thousand eyes are on her when she leaves the supermarket to go back home. The kits cost a fortune and although she could afford to pay for them, she'd have less money for the weekend ahead. Things are bad enough as they are without being skint as well. Besides, she knows the others do the same from time to time, putting something next to your till is common practice when a customer decides they don't want it after reaching the check-out, and it's too hard for the security guards or the supervisors to go round checking every single thing that goes missing. Most of it is just presumed stolen anyway. She hurries from the supermarket and makes her way onto the dual carriageway. Her legs are aching after another day spent mostly sitting, with only minimal breaks to go for a smoke or for dinner, and so she heads for the bus station, not wanting to pay for a bus home, but the walk back is too much to bear.

She imagines the kits burning a hole in her bag, not because they are stolen, but because of the implications they carry. She has decided to go through with it when she gets home, although her stomach churns at the thought. Back in her room she throws the bag onto her bed and goes for a shower. While washing herself she looks down at her stomach, wondering how long it takes for anything to show. She is sure she is getting fatter even now, and she pinches her hips to check for any undue expansion. Over tea she sits mostly in silence with Mark and her mother. Jason is not home again and that dominates proceedings, her mother constantly muttering to herself after putting his cottage pie into the microwave for later. Mark says nothing either. She tries asking him about his day at school but he gives only monosyllabic answers if he replies at all. And so she is left to her own thoughts as they race around her mind, making her feel light-headed. After tea she goes back to her room, puts some music on, and looks at the bag sitting waiting for her to make a decision, to take the next step and get it all over with. She has half a bottle of Taboo left from her birthday and she drinks deeply to try and drum up enough courage to go into the bathroom.

Half pissed, she cries into her pillow when she looks at the used tests on her bedside drawers. She's taken three of the four in the packets, but they're all positive. After the first one she took some hope from the bit in the instructions that said they aren't definite, that mistakes were possible. But when a second blue line appeared in the window of the next test she felt her insides disappear. She refuses to believe it. She feels hollow at the thought of it and thinks it can't be right. She has not changed, she does not feel any different, wouldn't she feel different? So she takes yet another one and the same thing happens again and she sobs heavily on her bed, using the pillow to stifle the noise. Her mother passes by outside and she stops herself from breathing until the footsteps make their way downstairs again. She wishes she could tell her mum about what is happening, but she knows she will kill her for what she has done. There are names for girls like her and her mother uses them a lot.

She finds it hard to sleep that night, even after finishing off the Taboo. She spends a fitful time in her bed, moving from one side to the other, hearing the television blaring downstairs and telling her mum she wants to be alone when she asks if she wants to come and watch. Mark is in the room next to her and she even considers telling him. She is desperate to confide in someone, but she cannot move. Jason does not come back and for that she is grateful, she knows what he would think. Her eyes blink open when she hears her dad come home the next morning after a late shift, her tears flowing again as she imagines his reaction. There are four missed calls on her phone from Dan, but she cannot see him just yet. A text message comes up asking where she is, but again she does not reply, and she begins to hate herself for ignoring him, knowing he will be angry and will want to know why she didn't answer her phone. Everything is piling up inside her head, recriminations look likely at every turn, and when she does manage to sleep, her dreams are filled with babies and childbirth. She can see herself in the hospital, alone, screaming as the baby comes out of her. The pain in her dream wakes her up and she grabs at her stomach, sitting up in bed and sweating, afraid of the future.

Mark is not far from tears when he finally gets on the bus home. He's never been so humiliated in his entire life and he despises those who have made him feel this way. After sprinting from the classroom, positive that people had guessed what had happened, sure that there is some tell-tale sign that he has a load of shit in his trousers, he had made it to a toilet without any spilling out down his leg. He cannot even find comfort in the silence of the toilets now that everyone is in their lessons. If only he had managed to hold on for ten more minutes, then excused himself, he could have been saved from what he was now going through. He shakes his head and the idea away. He is not at fault, it is them, they have made him like this, ashamed and alone. He takes his shoes and trousers off in one of the cubicles and drops the load nestling in his underpants into the bowl, realising now how much it stinks and wondering how he could have believed there was any chance of keeping it concealed. He wipes himself down and puts his trousers back on before washing out his underpants in one of the sinks. He feels that he now truly knows what degradation is like, thinking back to a history lesson he once had about kids who used to hide in toilets in concentration camps while people defecated all over them. Intense shame, self-pity, fear and loathing course through him all at once as he frantically rubs the dirt away with his thumbs, praying no one will come in and find him like this.

Once done, he scrubs at his hands with the malodorous nuggets of school regulation soap before wrapping the wet garment in with his games kit, hoping the smell of mud from his football boots will cover that emanating from his soiled underwear. Then he makes his excuses at the front reception, hoping he looks as ill as he feels, and thankfully he is told he can go home. He trudges down the path and out of the school gates thinking everything over, remembering the looks shot at him in the classroom when he had made his way out, and especially the look on the teacher's face. He is sure he saw recognition in her eyes and in some of the girls who sniggered as he reached his pathetic low in asking to leave the room. The teacher knew and they knew, the smell, the horror in his eyes, the pathetic excuse, how could they not know? He knows his ignominy will be extended to biblical proportions if he returns tomorrow, so he decides to take tomorrow off, unable to deal with what another day will hold for him if he does go back. Tomorrow is Friday and maybe, just maybe, the weekend will help people forget what has happened. He won't get a chance to go out tomorrow night if he is claiming to be unwell but he doesn't much feel like socialising anyway. Along with the shame comes hatred for those who have hounded him down until he has finally reached his own personal rock bottom. They have made him like this. It is not his fault, he is better than them, and yet they are winning the battle over him. And he despises them for it, every single one of them.

His contempt for his peers has already reached boiling point when two girls board the bus and sit behind him. His anger burns silently inside him while he listens to them making derogatory comments about people outside as the bus follows its route, ridiculing anyone they can.

'Look at that nobhead, what the fuck is he wearing?'

'And what about her, maungy bitch? I bet she reckons she's fucking hard or something. Look at clarinet girl, what a dork. Who the fuck carries a clarinet round with them in a case like that?'

'It's a pool cue you daft cow.'

'Oh. Well she's got stupid hair anyway.'

Then they start to take an interest in him.

'You don't mind if I lean over do yer?'

'He's not talking to you.'

'Don't you want to talk to me? Ere, you, why won't you talk to us?'

'I don't want to talk to you.'

'Why not, you might like it?'

'Don't be an ignorant bastard, you can talk to us. We won't bite, promise.'

'Do you really want to know why I don't want to talk to you?'

'Go on then.'

'Because I don't need to. There is absolutely nothing I want to talk to you about because I already know everything about you. I know you're both called something like Donna or Debbie and although you act really tough, it's just because you're scared out of your wits about the fact that you know you're going nowhere. It's like a stupid defence mechanism, taking the piss out of other people before they can take the piss out of you. You act like you don't care about anything and that nothing can touch you, but the fact is you're scared shitless because you know how little you have to offer. You talk louder than anyone else, hoping to be a bit different, cause a bit of a stir, because at the end of the day you know you've got nothing and never will. You'll have a few kids, probably by different blokes, none of which will give a shit about you and will probably dump you the minute you're up the duff. They'll probably beat you up too and you'll moan and claim off the social because you won't have a qualification to call your own because you don't want to look like you care about school because that would leave you wide open to abuse. And you'll never really be in love even though you might eventually find a decent bloke who doesn't hit you and will look after your kids because you'll reject him and cheat on him with the bastards you've been with before because you don't think you deserve any better until he can't take any more and he'll go off and leave you alone with three kids and a face screwed up by too much beer and fags. You'll be fat and alone and you'll never enjoy sex because you'll never let yourself go enough to care about the person on top of you. And you'll complain about how you never got the breaks and swear at your kids, who'll turn into the same sad fuck that you are now and you won't even try to control them and the circle of your stupid little life will go on and on and on. That's why I don't want to talk to you. Because I'll never be the same and I don't want to be.'

Mark stood to get off the bus despite being nowhere near his house. He just wanted to be away from them, away from everyone, and he didn't turn to look at the girls again even after one of them landed a gob of phlegm on his back.

In the bathroom, Jason leaned against the wall over the toilet, smiling to himself. What a day. How the hell can anyone ever want to work when this is the alternative? A day spent in the pub with your mates, shagging your girlfriend in the park after nicking a bottle of vodka and now everyone smoking dope and doing buckets back at Craig's house. And above it all there's no need to think about going to some stupid factory tomorrow morning where some bastard shouts at you all day for not nearly enough money. This is the fucking life, not working, just drinking and smoking and shagging and pissing. Jason looks down at his knob and winks – done the business again. If he thought he fancied Nicola before it doesn't even compare to what he thinks now. When they'd been running after the others she'd stopped suddenly and pulled him into the park, straight behind some bushes, pulled his trousers down and dropped to her knees. He'd been so shocked he hadn't even registered what was happening for a few moments. And when he finally realised what was actually going on, he'd just stood there in awe, watching her head moving back and forward, not hurting him once like some girls did. Then he'd lowered himself down onto her and they'd shagged on the grass, bareback for God's sake. What a first time. If that was the sign of things to come, Jason felt he was going to be a very happy man.

He shook himself dry and had another look at what was in his hands. His vision was a bit blurred, but it looked like there were some little marks around the foreskin. He peered closer, closing one eye to do so, and saw there were some little bumps on the skin. Not many, maybe five or six, but they were definitely there. They were only tiny things, like very small spots or something, but they looked pretty fucking terrifying on the end of his knob. He flushed the toilet and turned round to sit on the closed seat. There they were, all around the edge of his foreskin, near the tip, and when he pulled it back a bit they looked even more like spots.

'What the fuck?' he said aloud. Suddenly he started to get very worried. And angry. He immediately thought back to having sex with Nicola and whether those marks had been there before. He was sure they hadn't. What had the bitch given him? How could he have been so stupid as to believe her stories about not having shagged that many lads? She'd had blokes crawling all over her at school and probably still did now. She could have anything. The spots suddenly sprouted and grew larger right in front of his eyes. What if these were the precursor to something far more awful? What if he had AIDS? Jason had started sweating and he washed his face in the basin next to him. Looking at himself in the mirror, everything seemed back to normal again and he started wondering if he had seen the marks at all. But when he sat back down and opened his jeans they were still there, looking even more prominent.

'Are you all right in there Jay?' Johnny said from outside the door.

'Yeh,' said Jason, trying to keep the rising panic out of his voice.

'Not chucking a whitey or anything?'

'No, I'll be out in a minute.'

Jason's mind was all over the place, but he managed to calm down for a moment and think about what he could do. What if he didn't get this off Nicola, what if it was some bird he'd had before? Then again, what if it was nothing at all, what if it was just because he hadn't had a shower recently – what if it was just some dirt that had got under the skin and started a rash? Oh please God, let it just be a rash. Johnny's mum worked in the GU clinic at the infirmary and because of that Jason knew a bit about this sort of thing. There was no point in getting all worked up about something or blaming anyone for anything until he knew for definite what was actually going on. He finally opened the door and made his way back downstairs to where the others were still smoking away. Nicola passed him a joint and he inhaled deeply, wanting to forget everything he'd just been thinking and try and focus on what was happening around him now.

'We're going to have to go on another run soon,' said Johnny.

'Oh by the way lads, cheers for putting me onto that bloke in Scholes. He's got me some quality gear recently,' said Craig.

Jason suddenly developed an itch in his crotch, right on the end of his penis. He shifted about uncomfortably next to Nicola, one arm around her, the other hand passing the joint back to her before scratching himself.

'What's up with you, you got crabs or something?' said Johnny when he saw what Jason was doing.

'He'd better fucking not have,' said Nicola, but she is joking, her hand squeezing Jason's arm affectionately. Jason smiled at her but this action made him even more panicky. He can't have got it off her, he only shagged her about an hour or so ago, it wouldn't happen that quickly. When he was in the kitchen getting another beer later, Johnny came in. Nicola had gone home as she was working in the morning and just Craig, Jason, Johnny and Louise remained, playing on Craig's PlayStation.

'Your mum still works at that clinic doesn't she?' said Jason.

'Yeh. Why, you thinking of going?' Johnny said, smiling.

'Am I fuck. No, our Mark's doing a school project and he wanted me to ask you if your mum had any books about STD's.'

'I can have a look for you.'

'Cheers mate. It wouldn't surprise me if the little bugger's worried he's caught something wanking about that Stacey over the road. He's a dozy shite when it comes to women.'

If it's a boy, then it'll be James, if it's a girl, Chloe. Or Emily, or Ryan. There are so many names to choose from. She took a book from Tesco's today, a book of children's names, and she sits in her bedroom reading it while her hair dries ready for tonight. Another Friday night, but this one will be different for so many reasons. She'll have to turn down the offers of drinks, have to make excuses for not wanting as much alcohol as usual. She'll have to have a few to avoid suspicion, but when she goes to buy the round she'll make sure hers is just orange juice, that way they won't be able to tell whether it's got vodka in it or not. When the others buy drinks, she'll have a half here, a Bacardi Breezer there, besides, she'll need a couple inside her if she's to tell Dan. And she is going to tell him tonight. She's worried about how he will react but he has to know. She has decided she is going to keep it, the names have persuaded her to do that. And they'll go out to the park together, the three of them, pushing the pram along and then when it's older, the buggy. She can still go to college, her mum will look after the baby while she goes to night school and prepares herself for the future. She has no idea what he will say, whether he will stay with her or not, but she thinks he will. He's not the type to just leave – they have been through too much together already, there is no way he'd just desert her.

They start the night in Embargo, her and Vicky and Collette

and Jane from work. All the others they asked from Tesco's are either with their husbands or boyfriends or looking after their kids, but even that doesn't faze her. Nights out round Wigan are losing their appeal now she has Dan. All she gets is hassle from blokes, pinching her arse, trying to buy her drinks, trying to get off with her when all she wants to do is dance with her mates. It doesn't happen just yet, not at the start of the night, but she knows that later, in the Springbok, there will be some sweaty lad putting his arms around her from behind on the dance floor, trying to get her to move with him, pushing his unwanted advances against her back. She would be happy just staying in now and then, watching videos with Dan, or going to the cinema. He goes out with his mates and she goes out with hers and they meet up later on, but only after about twenty other lads have tried to grope her. From the Embargo they go to Berkeley Square, at the top of King Street, then to Ibiza, then to Springbok. King Street is strange even to her these days, new bars open all the time, new clubs spring up out of nowhere. Her mates have been going round town for a lot longer than she has and they always go on about how different it is now, how it's more packed than ever before as bar after bar opens and people come to drink from all around.

She sees a few girls she used to go to school with up on the balcony in Berkeley and they tell her all about the men in their lives, the babies they've had, the wedding or kid they're expecting. She doesn't think they sound stupid anymore and she feels like she is happy being just like them, talking about boys and babies and houses and jobs. Dan meets them in Springbok later, arms encircling her from behind, Denise just about to brush another one off her until she realises it is finally who she wants to see. They dance, they drink, Denise's worries about having alcohol diminishing by the minute, besides, every time she asks for orange, Dan makes sure there's at least one shot in there too. She isn't even afraid of when the right moment to tell him will be, her plans out of her head for the moment as she just enjoys what is going on around her. He takes her to their alley near the swimming baths at about one o'clock, following her down the rusty metal steps and into the darkness, ready for a bit of action before the chore of getting a taxi home. As he puts his hand up her skirt, pulling down her knickers with one hand while his other goes underneath her top, something finally clicks within her and she remembers what she has to say. He stands there, out of breath, not angry at her rejection, staring at her with lust burning in his eyes that are picked out by the streetlamp above. He thinks they are about to carry on any minute, until she drops the bombshell.

He can't believe it at first. 'Are you sure?' he asks. 'How do you know? Have you checked? When did it happen? How did it happen?' He is shocked but then sees the fear in her eyes, the anxiety that he is going to reject her and he starts smiling. 'I can't believe it,' he says. 'I can't fucking believe it.' He grabs her, lifts her up in his arms, twirls her round, trying to avoid the bins behind her and the empty cans and litter scattered at their feet. She is so happy and so relieved she starts crying and he kisses her face all over, telling her he loves her, saying he can't wait, saying he wants to be with her forever. He has no doubt in his mind that anything is amiss and she will never let him know any different, never let anything go wrong. He is the man for her and she will hold on at all costs, as though clinging to a cliff edge.

He had yet another bath this morning but it's made no difference. He still feels dirty.

His mum was surprised at first when he came home early yesterday, but was sympathetic when he told her he wasn't well. She said he smelled a bit. He's got the whole day to himself, his dad asleep upstairs, his mum working at the Hospice, and so he tries to read a bit, but his memories of being at school flood back to him and so he watches telly instead. He can still see the faces of the girls near the door when he left the classroom, the sniggering beginning already. And then the faces of the girls on the bus, their hoop earrings ridiculously large, their grotesquely young painted-on sneers. Denise tried to talk to him over tea last night but he couldn't bear to look at either her or his mum. Thankfully his mum was too busy fretting over Jason to take much of an interest in him. He hasn't come home today either and she was still too distracted to disbelieve his continued illness and allowed him to stay off school with barely an argument. Her worrying continues when she comes home from work that afternoon and his dad says Jason has still not returned. And when Mark quietly pulls the back door to, she doesn't bat an eyelid when he heads out and up the street, wanting to be on his own for an hour or so by the ponds in the woods.

He wants to think of her, only of her, but even she is tainted, taken by another. He thinks back to the park and Georgie, remembering how her bush had looked in the dark, hairy and unappealing, and yet he had wanted her all the same. He longs to do it just once, get it over with, feel different to the way he does now. He does not know whether or not to believe his friends when they talk about their experiences, but in some cases he has no reason for dispute. He has seen the way girls look at Jamie, noticed how they have talked to him only to gather information about his friend. One time when Claire Green came over to talk to him in a chemistry lesson, sneaking over when the teacher had left the room, Mark had immediately began fantasising about situations involving her: she was coming over to ask him out, or to find out where he was going that night, wanting to meet him later on. But instead she had asked about Jamie, where he was going, whether he fancied her or not. Thinking back on it now, he feels even more deflated than ever.

He has to get away, be somewhere where people don't know him, won't make fun of him, but will want to do what he wants to do: talk about books, go to the pictures, want him in their bed. He imagines a cellist, a Russian one, who has come over to study music at Oxford. She will play in the corner of his room while he writes an essay on *Lord of the Flies*, his masterpiece. And then later, when the candles have burned down low, she will put aside her instrument and come over to him, exhausted from his work. She will understand his academic need, his thirst for knowledge, but she will want to help him to rest when he becomes weary:

'You must rest a while. Take me to bed and forget it all for a few hours.' He will lay her down and they will make love three, four times, watching in awe as dawn fills the room with a red hue, while the windows steam up with sweat and dew. They will walk together by the river in the early morning, not talking, just holding hands and listening to the birds as they too begin to awaken. And the sun will rise above the spires as church bells ring out and he will lie in her lap on a grassy verge, her hand stroking his hair, his mind nowhere to be found.

He sits on the remains of the old mill they tore down years ago. Concrete boulders and broken bricks lie scattered across the hill, and he throws stones down into the stagnant green ponds below him. In the near distance he can hear people applauding as a cricket match is played out at the Parish Hall, and faint laughter grates on him like a jagged knife. He carries on throwing stones and trying to block out the sounds from all around until he sees some people heading along the concrete walkway that runs beside the furthest pond. There's a few of them, no one he recognises, and they're all laughing and carrying bottles of cider. Not tonight. He cannot face anyone tonight, and besides, he could be on for a beating rather than a piss up if it's someone he doesn't know. So he gets up and walks back home, past the truck yard and the horse-dotted fields and over the railway across the road back down Enfield Street. There is movement all around, people getting ready for another Friday night on the town or around Pemberton. There are lights flashing in The Railway's windows and the sign outside says: 'Karaoke Tonight'. He takes a quick look at a couple of girls as they walk past, obviously heading down to where he's just come from to meet up with others and get pissed. Denise is getting ready to go out when he gets back and God knows where his mum and dad are. He goes to his room and listens to music for a while, eventually falling asleep after drinking the two cans of beer he's officially allowed on a Friday.

It's dark when he wakes up, but it can't be too late as he can still hear the telly downstairs. The streetlamps outside cast his room with an orange glow. It is not his room officially, he and

Jason have always shared, but his brother spends so much time away he can feel as though it is his own personal space. He wipes his eyes and sits up, looking at his alarm clock to see it's well past midnight. Then, through his open curtains, he sees the light across the road. She's in. Either that or her mum is cleaning her room again. He rests his chin on the windowsill and looks into her bedroom. It is her, she's back early from wherever it is she's been that night. She moves around, messing about with unseen objects behind the walls. She doesn't look happy, in fact the mascara lines on her face give away that she's been crying. Mark flinches when she throws a cushion against the far wall, colliding with the black and white poster of James Dean. She likes those old film stars and Mark watches old films as often as possible to see if he can emulate them in some way. She never notices, but he tries all the same.

And then the glory begins. Part of the right curtain is covering his usual line of view, but he can still see enough. First her top comes off to reveal a bulging black bra and her expanding stomach. He can see to the top of her thighs if she stands in the right position and he waits anxiously to see if he will get any more tonight, dropping his jeans at the thought of it. Her stomach fascinates him, the massive expanse of peachy flesh, the belly button protruding from its previously hidden domain. He continues stroking even when she turns around and disappears from sight. She hasn't closed the curtains yet and that means there is more to come. She must have put some music on as she starts to sway from one side of the room to the other, arranging things, disappearing for a few moments here and there before continuing her exotic dance right in front of him. He imagines that she knows he is watching, that she dances just for him, lowering her skirt to the floor before rising again and starting to unhook her bra. Mark cannot believe it when her hands suddenly stop what she is doing and she disappears again. He slows his movement until she comes back with a phone in her hand. She rests against the windowsill, talking animatedly to whoever is on the other end of the line, and Mark continues, his eyes hooked on her cleavage. Her face begins to redden and her chest heaves up and down as she starts shouting. Suddenly she throws the phone behind her before turning back to the windowsill and crying. After a few moments she composes herself and looks out of the window. Mark stares straight back at her, wondering if her eyes really can pick him out from the darkness of his room. She slowly unhooks her bra and her breasts, which have grown ever larger since she became pregnant, fall out, majestic and free. He ejaculates at last as she reaches over to close one curtain, then the other, bringing the show to an end with the taste of her tears fresh in his mouth.

I've heard them talk I know what they're saying about it being a shotgun wedding but I'll tell you what it is it's just jealousy that's all I don't care what they think I know that they were going to get married anyway and that's good enough for me just because she's having a kid now it doesn't make any difference just speeded things up that's all they were always talking about it before she knew she was pregnant just because their daughter's about to drop again and not a man anywhere near to take responsibility not like Dan I mean I know he has his faults and everything but at least he's got a job and at least he's standing by her not like any of the blokes she's ever been with I know she's only young but what difference does it make these days as long as they've got jobs and can look after it I'll always be there of course I've often said to my Frank that I've missed having a baby about and besides I was only nineteen myself when I was pregnant with our Jason and he's turned out all right well they all have I've got no complaints especially the way you see some of these kids turning out these days it's scandalous I heard only the other day of a seventy-seven year old woman being beaten nearly to death in Worsley Mesnes by a group of young girls and what for all for the twenty quid she had in her handbag and if it's not one thing it's another there's a girl who our Mark goes to school with she's just got herself into trouble for stealing from the petty cash just standing there in school still in her uniform and everything and she just pops her hand over the counter in reception and has it away with the tin you wouldn't believe what some of 'em get up to these days it's shocking I mean it makes you not want to even watch the news when all there is is death and stealing and old folk being beaten up for twenty quid and if it's not that they're stealing mobile phones it makes you wonder whether or not it's even right to bring another child into the world but you want to see Dan he's getting all excited about being a father I can tell he was funny the other day the look on his face when I said he still can't stay over until there's a gold band next to that diamond I told him I don't mind some things but I'm still old fashioned in my own way but he's a nice lad though he's been buying cuddly toys and clothes and everything and he's done that room up a treat painted it blue with clouds on and everything well they know it's a boy after she went in for a scan it sounds as though everything's going well and Denise has never been happier of course she's not supposed to drink but I said a glass of wine here and there never hurt anyone I smoked all the way through all of mine and they never had any problems apart from our Mark who had those early problems with his ears but the doctors were right when they said he'd grow out of it eventually and she's got to have some fun on her hen do oh it'll be grand we're all off to Blackpool for the night and staying over in a B&B by the seafront she can't wait I can tell she's a bit worried about him and his stag night what with his mates but I told her not to worry I mean he wouldn't be male if he couldn't cut loose every now and then I mean God knows we do our best Jean but you can't change 'em if they don't want to be changed and you probably wouldn't want 'em even if they did anyway our Jason's going an' all so it's not like he'll let anything go overboard he might make out like him and Denise don't get on but I can tell how much he cares really I can't tell whether he's more made up than she is half the time when they talk about the baby he's itching to be an uncle of course our Mark is as well but it's really brought something out in Jason he seems happier than ever mind you a bit of that's to do with the fact that he's courting this girl he used to go to school with I'll tell you what he acts like a hard case sometimes but he's a soft touch when it comes to girls he bought her flowers the other day he didn't think I'd seen him but I did going into the Esso garage in Pemberton and picking out a bunch for her and it's only been about four months mind you it's about time he settled down anyway I've seen the types he hangs round with sometimes and that time when he brought that little tart Donna Entwhistle back to our house well I nearly killed him for that he tried telling me there was no one in the room with him the next morning but I made out like I'd gone out and caught him trying to sneak her out the back door the bugger I mean really messing about with dirty little slappers like Donna Entwhistle you'd think he'd know better by his age in some ways you can't blame her what with the way her mother dresses when all she's doing is going to the shops animal print tops and skirts up to her neck you'd think she was fourteen not forty-five but this Nicola seems nice not like any of the others he's ever been with polite and clever she works for HSBC in Wigan and reckons she might be manager one day unless she does something else and he's got another job too in a computer warehouse he's been there for over two months now he's cleaned up his act that boy I'm proud of him he gets himself up and showers himself when he gets home always trying to look his best for when she comes round I'll tell you I should buy her a drink for what she's done for him two months is longer than his last three jobs put together and he even says he likes this one well I've always said you have to be happy in your work but as for our Mark though God knows when he's going to get himself a girlfriend I mean I know he's only young and everything but all he does is mope around the house or lock himself in his bedroom he thinks I don't know what he's doing half the time but I've heard him slapping away they must think we were born yesterday some of these kids I ask him what he's doing and he says his homework but I know what's really going on Jason was the same but at least he went out as well not our Mark he's still got his big ideas about living somewhere else and becoming God knows what it's a doctor one week and a lawyer the next always dreaming that boy always dreaming

Winter

Jason watches the kids playing on the fields next to the Labour club. Little Danny is wrestling with Ryan, another lad from the estate behind. They're grappling with each other as they try to get to the football nearby. Even though it's December it's a sunny day and Jason puts his face back for a moment to take in the warmth. You can never tell what the weather's going to be like, never understand it at all. It's the middle of winter and all of a sudden it goes hot on you.

He's a cute kid Danny, small but perfectly made, with thick blonde hair covering his head almost in a Beatles style. He wins the battle over Ryan and runs triumphantly over to the ball, kicking it along as Ryan runs awkwardly after him. They're both six years old and while Jason likes watching them messing about, he doesn't understand how Johnny copes when he calls him his own. He isn't Johnny's at all. The father is some bloke called Chris who Louise knew when she was at school but now wants nothing to do with her. Jason is pretty sure he could never look after someone else's kid the way Johnny does, especially when he is constantly undermined by Louise's mum. Johnny will try and tell Danny off and Louise's mum berates him for doing so. 'How dare you talk to him like that,' she's said in the past. She's never directly said 'he's not even yours', but the implication is there for all to see.

He's not Johnny's son, but he's been good enough to take on a single mum and treats Danny as though he is his own. If I were him I'd tell them all to get stuffed. I'll never fall into that trap and I'll never let a girl trap me. If anything was to happen I'd take the consequences but I'm not about to go taking on someone else's responsibility. And it's not like Louise helps either. She just sits there, drinking or smoking, paying little attention to what's going on, as though making up for lost time when she was carrying, although she probably didn't restrict herself even then. Fuck all that, Jason decides, if a girl's stupid enough to get knocked up, let her and the bloke suffer, not me. My life's complicated enough.

Things are still going well with Nicola, but Jason is beginning to wonder what's supposed to happen next. He once went out with someone for over a year, but that was when he was a lot younger and didn't know anything about anything. She was called Janine and he'd shat all over her, sleeping with any bird he could find. When she'd found out she'd gone apeshit, dumping him but only after she'd cut his cheek with the sovereign ring she always used to wear. He's not been anything like that this time around, hasn't slept with anyone else while he's been with her, doesn't even really want to, but still he'd had a problem with his knob. If it's not one thing it's another, and for Jason it had been warts.

He doesn't have them anymore. He's been to the clinic a few times and got rid of the little bastards, but the book he borrowed from Johnny's mum and what the doctor told him has had him worrying at least once a day ever since. It was so embarrassing when he'd gone to the clinic, dropping his trousers in front of another bloke. He'd shrivelled up almost into a little ball when the doctor had started prodding him about, taking a really close look at the offending object. It's warts all right, he'd said, but Jason had worked that out for himself after reading that book. It'd turned his stomach looking at all the pictures in there, a description of each disease on one side and nine pictures on the other. Double page spreads for things like AIDS. Dicks and fannies all infected with one thing or another stared back at him from the pages with infested, pus filled scabs, ulcers and spots and warts and crabs and every conceivable disgusting foul looking thing on the planet. He'd picked up as many condoms as he could after that, telling Nicola they had to be careful from now on, having to grit his teeth when he said what happened in the park couldn't happen again, they couldn't be lucky forever. He dreamed about syphilis and herpes and gonorrhoea and chlamydia and warts and scabies and hepatitis and yaws and AIDS, the symptoms and descriptions, and most of all the pictures still fresh in his head. Thank God he'd got cleared up before she went on the pill.

She hadn't noticed the warts, they'd only been little things and all that they'd had to do was freeze them off. It hurt like a bastard at the time but Jason hadn't cared, had almost invited the pain so that in some way he could feel purged of his crime by undergoing such a punishment. They told him he had to tell anyone he'd slept with in the last however how long. But there'd only been Nicola, and that other bird that Friday night. He didn't know where she was and there was no way he was telling Nicola. They'd gone now, and that was all that mattered. Just like when he'd been younger and had warts on his hands, they hadn't come back, and neither would these. No one needed to know except him and the doctor, and that was the end of that. He's not messing this up. Even though the thought of being with Nicola for forever frightens him, the thought of not being with her is much worse. He looks up and sees Danny and Ryan having a bit of a fight. Johnny gets up from sitting next to him and runs over to break it up, giving them both a quick slap. He's lucky Louise is not around to see him disciplining them. Not that she'd do anything, probably just shout at them in-between taking drags from her cigarette, not actually moving, just waiting until Johnny gets involved and then having a go at him for it afterwards.

Jason wants kids, but his own, not some other fucker's. He has no intention of taking on a mess that's got nothing to do with him. Pot Noodle families – just add father. Mind you, there aren't that many girls about who haven't already had at least one kid.

You always see them, pushing prams, smoking away – never worked a day in their life and probably never will. They either claim off the state, or, if they're lucky, some other poor sod who's daft enough to take them and a kid on. Johnny has fallen into the trap head first. He met Louise about a year ago and already he's expected to stay home sometimes while she goes out and enjoys herself. It takes the piss the way she has him tied down already. Jason always asks to see what he's up to, if he fancies a few beers or a proper full on night round town. Most of the time he gets a positive response, but there are the odd occasions when Johnny has to stay home playing dad. And playing is all it is. He's not nearly old enough to have to do what he does. Of course there are people even younger than him doing the same thing, but Johnny doesn't have to be like that. He could be doing what he wanted but instead he's ruled by some bint who isn't worth it and a kid that isn't even his.

ASDA is packed on a Saturday. The River Douglas meanders alongside the car park, black and sparkling, as cars in slow-moving queues search for places to stop. Even though it's open twenty-four hours a day now and people can go whenever they want, everyone is still stuck in the routine of doing their weekly shopping at the weekend. But it's the easiest place for Denise to get baby clothes and so she and Dan have to make their way through the crowds wandering about aimlessly, as though deliberately trying to get in their way. The fact that it's near Christmas doesn't help either, but they don't have any choice. Dan doesn't get many Saturdays off so they have to go now and Denise is determined to get everything she needs so they don't have to come back in a hurry. Not that he even wants to be there in the first place. The baby isn't due for ages yet and he doesn't see the point, can't they do it later? When later though? Do it now and then it's out the way. Denise has always loved Christmas shopping and this year there's even more reason to look forward to the festivities. She's been saving her money meticulously since finding out about the baby. The nights in she visualised with Dan, sitting there watching videos, have become a reality, and any small things she might need she takes from Tesco's whenever she gets a chance. Dan is still not allowed to sleep in her bedroom but he often spends nights on the couch, and she sneaks down to see him in the middle of the night when she hears her parents snoring. Her dad is back on days again so they both go up to bed about half ten and she comes back down the minute the familiar sound of their sleep comes through her wall.

The only downside is that she is often tired and that she needs to go to the loo all the time. Dan gets a bit tetchy with her, especially when she doesn't want sex, but she tries to keep him occupied as much as possible. She watched a programme on daytime TV years ago all about men who went with other women while their wives were pregnant and it has stuck with her ever since. If she has an ounce of energy left after work she makes sure she performs for him. She trusts him, but at the end of the day he's a man and all men will stray if they're not satisfied. Her hen do is all set, Vicky has made the arrangements for a night out in Blackpool on Boxing Day and she can't wait. There's fifteen of them altogether, her mum is coming and so are a lot of the girls from work. This Christmas is going to be the best ever, dinner with her family on the day itself, then her hen night on Boxing Day. Dan is just going round Wigan for his stag night, but he's making it an all-day thing to make up for it. She was worried about what might happen, strippers and all that, but Jason will be there and that puts her mind at ease slightly. She knows Dan loves her and believes him when he says he doesn't want anyone else. Besides, it's not like her hen do is going to be all sitting around talking about shopping. She knows well enough how to have a good time when the occasion calls for it, even in her present state, and what bigger occasion could there be than her last night as a free woman?

Her mum has given her a list of things to buy and as they walk down the aisles together, she is already imagining herself walking down the Church aisle with him. The wedding is set for early February and while she is slightly disappointed that she will be showing on her wedding day, her mum has told her in no uncertain terms that she will not be giving birth to a bastard. Mind you, she is four months down the line now and she is still not showing that much. Her mum had always called her a sickly child, even before she had been threatened by anaemia all those years ago. She's nothing like that now, but she is still hoping she can keep most of her bump hidden on the big day. They were lucky that the Church had a cancellation. St Matthews is a popular place for weddings and she cannot wait for the ceremony and especially the pictures. There are trees galore outside the ornate wooden doors and loads of chances for good photo opportunities. Her mum has found a place that specialises in bigger wedding dresses and they have told her that making her stomach as flattering as possible should not be a problem.

A bumper pack of frozen pies goes into the trolley as she pushes it around and Dan collects the items on the list. She needs to go over to the clothes bit to get a shirt for Mark and an Oasis CD for Jason. She knows he hasn't got the latest one yet and is hoping he's as lazy as usual and doesn't buy it before she can. She's getting a big bottle of whisky for her dad and a Dionne Warwick CD for her mum. After Dan loads the trolley with the last of the beer her mum has budgeted for, case after case of lager and numerous boxes of wine, they pay for the stuff and head back to his car. Everyone seems in a happy mood. The sun is shining and cheers ring out from the JJB Stadium where Latics are playing. Someone's just scored and Denise hopes it's Wigan or her dad will be in a right nark later. Back at home and the supplies are unloaded, her mum jolly with the weather and the fact that it's nearly Christmas, even Mark is smiling and she playfully twists his nose to take his attention away from the book he's reading. They drive to Ashurst Beacon, drop the car off at the car park near the golf course, and head up the grassy hill towards the stone beacon itself. Denise can't manage though, her legs feel heavy after shopping all day, and so they just sit on the embankment, looking out over the trees to Blackpool on the horizon. It has always amazed her how you can see so far from this spot and she gets Dan to point the Tower out to her. She gets it and then looks out over the sea instead, the sun glinting across it making it silver. There is a chill in the air and Dan puts his arm around her shoulder.

Nearly Christmas break. Mark can't wait. School hasn't been too bad recently, a lot of work as the exam clock ticks down towards Armageddon, but he can spend more time revising now he's quit bottle snatching at the Parish Hall. He has made sure there have been no repeats of what happened in English. He usually goes to the toilet well before he leaves for school, or, if he is absolutely desperate, there is another toilet he has found by the woodwork rooms that is nowhere near the rest of the school and is generally unlocked. No one mentioned what had happened when he returned after the weekend. A couple of his mates said he hadn't looked well. Everyone smelled the smell but the consensus of opinion is that he was just farting a lot. From that moment on Mark resolved not to worry so much in the future, there was no point. He'd spent the whole weekend in agony and for what?

They've been acting out a musical in drama recently, *Anything Goes.* There's no production at the end of it, but it's a good laugh all the same. And he's been getting on very well with a girl called Sam in his drama class, talking to her and messing about. His mates reckon she fancies him, but Mark is not counting his chickens just yet. She's nice though, with dark hair and glasses and a nice smell. He is pretty sure she is well out of his league, but she doesn't seem to mind sitting next to him or whispering jokes in his ear when the teacher isn't looking. The lads who normally take the piss seem to look at him in a different light now he's started hanging about with her as well.

She's clever, but she's good looking too, the get-out clause some girls have when they earn good marks in school. It doesn't matter what you look like as a lad, you are a swot if you try at all. But with girls it is only the ugly or plain ones who are chastised for doing well in their studies. The good looking ones can do whatever they like, mostly because the lads will follow them around anyway. Mark has often despaired of this. When he has talked to a clever, good looking girl before, he has always got on well with them. That is, until another lad turns up. Then they've always changed the way they act, dumbed themselves down to fit in, and he hasn't spoken to them since. But then one day, totally out of the blue, he starts to get accepted himself. Something happens to him that has never happened before. He is given a detention. He is walking along the corridor when a younger kid pushes him out of the way as he runs in the opposite direction. Without thinking, Mark calls after him, 'Watch where you're going you dozy fuckwit!' And that's all it takes. He hadn't seen Mr Hall standing next to him at the time and as he turned to carry on to class, he was grabbed by the arm and marched to the headmaster's office.

He was dreading what his parents would say and he gets a roasting when his mum signs the slip. However, what happens after that makes it all worthwhile. Slowly but surely he becomes a part of things at school that he had previously been excluded from. He still does not totally belong, after all, he still tries to do well, but the bullying peters out and he even manages to go through whole days without being bothered. The harder lads who used to kick him or spit at him or call him names when he walked past either say nothing or actually say, 'All right Mark.' He gets even closer to Sam, her and her mates sometimes sit with him and his mates in the yard at breaks. He no longer gets picked on for no reason at all. Of course there are exceptions to the rule, it is not like he has suddenly become popular, but he is tolerated to an extent that he never even dreamed would be possible before. He gets another detention, for swearing again, and then he even has the good fortune to be rebuked while standing outside the classroom with the others, waiting to go in. One of the most feared teachers in the school comes over and asks him right in front of everyone if he went on the school roof that dinnertime. He had, he'd been getting a football down, but he had taken a set of ladders without asking permission. For this, he has to spend another Thursday after school in one of the classrooms writing out the school rules again and again for an hour, but he doesn't care. The whole class had erupted into laughter when the teacher had gone away again and Mark felt a part of things in a way he had never done before. It is not like he is going to get expelled or suspended like some lads who go too far, but these little excursions outside the rules bring him some small credibility, enough to make his hours at school happier than ever before.

Stacey is back with her husband to be. It's four months since the night she grabbed his arse at her hen do but she's still not married. Mark overheard his mum talking and it sounded like they cancelled the whole thing after he hit her on a night out. His mum said she was going the same way as Tracy next door – she'd dropped her third kid about a month ago and once again there was no father in sight. Somehow they must have patched things up though as Stacey's bloke is very much back in evidence, dropping her off at her house, his car rocking from side to side with their passionate farewells. His mum said she's due in January and they can't get married before then so there'll be four bastards in the street. She said Stacey was just the same as all the others, young and deluded and selfish and stupid. Mark stopped listening at that point.

She would never be the same as anyone, not Stacey. He might like Sam and a few of the other girls at school, but it will never be anything compared to how he feels about Stacey. He fancied her the minute she moved in. He can still remember the day the removal vans turned up on their street, curtains twitching from one end to the other as people tried for a quick glimpse of the new neighbours. She wasn't exciting just because she was something new, he was struck by her beauty from the minute he laid eyes on her. Big heels, a short red skirt, a black top with purple bra straps showing, and that shocking white hair. They had only moved from another part of Wigan and she had already been engaged, but he had wanted her straight away. While Tracy had greasy hair and spots and fat rolling out from under too small T-shirts, Stacey was like a model. He is back on the scene and so she spends a lot of time away from her house, but Mark is always watching whenever she returns. He cannot wait for Christmas and New Year, when everyone rolls out into the street at midnight and does the conga. In the past he's always been too shy to grab onto her in the dancing line, but he makes an early resolution to do so this year as he settles down to Romeo and Juliet by lamplight.

'Pass us your glass lad and I'll fill you up.'

'Frank, don't give him so much wine, he's only fifteen.'

'Don't talk nonsense woman, it's Christmas Day. Besides, he's not long off sixteen.'

'He won't be sixteen for four months yet.'

'For goodness sake, what does it matter? If the lad can't have a drink now, when can he?'

He was made redundant a week ago and he's only just managing to keep his anger hidden. It's Christmas Day though and he has to, for the kids' and Lil's sake, if not his own. He wants to smash things up, pour paint remover over his former manager's car, but he has to keep his emotions in check. One hundred and thirty-two men out of work just before Christmas, it beggars belief anyone could have the audacity. Everyone at the plant had known the time was coming, that for some men their job wouldn't last beyond the New Year, but the idea and half-promises of first in, last out had turned out to be a fantasy made up by men whose jobs and six-figure salaries were safe. He'd worked there for the last nineteen years and you would hardly have guessed it the ease with which he was tossed aside. The pay-out he received was okay, but could have been better. It does mean that he doesn't have to worry about getting another job straight away, unlike some poor bastards who've been left out in the cold literally this year. It isn't just about that though. Frank's been working solid since he was sixteen and he doesn't know what else to do. He liked working at Heinz, he liked the people he worked with. He'd worked his way up from the shop floor to being a supervisor and now they were just discarding him, filling his job and those of many others with a younger generation. They've got degrees, but there's no counting for experience. Frank knows those machines, the workings, the procedures, like the back of his hand. But give a snot-nosed kid a piece of paper from some fancy institution and it's cheerio lads, on your way now. Denise's wedding is the main worry, but they've got savings, and Dan's father has said he wants to make sure he pays his way as well. Frank's not so proud he won't take money off others. Besides, he's only in his forties, there are plenty of other jobs out there for a man like him, willing to work, with experience behind him. Come the New Year and it'll be a new start. Even his old Christmas dilemma about who to watch on Boxing Day, Latics or Wigan, was alleviated by the formation of Superleague and the Rugby League season being switched from winter to summer years ago. The traditional Boxing Day battles between Wigan and Saints continued as friendlies for a time but now they too had been phased out. Latics were playing too far away this year for travel to be practical, so all he planned to do was get himself in front of the nearest telly at quarter to five and watch the scores come in.

'Merry Christmas, sup up everyone.'

He's going to make it a merry Christmas too, he's determined to do that much. Fuck the lot of these corporate bastards, if they want to sell their souls to the devil it's got nothing to do with him. He's got money in his account, food on the table and drink in his hand, a loving wife and three kids. He's heard they're taking on at some factory just off Enfield Street and he's planning to have a look as soon as possible. Or there's the industrial estate out at Haydock. He likes the idea of working there and being able to go the races whenever he feels like it. No, things are never as bad as they first look. Lil was up in arms when he was laid off, she thought it should have been last in, first out, but it never works like that in real life, whether it should or not. He used to feel like Arthur Seaton, never letting the bastards grind him down. But he hasn't got the energy or ability to turn his anger against the system anymore. Besides, he's been in the system so long he feels a part of it, worked his way up from humble beginnings and even had a chance to run the show in his own way. And the system had turned on him, sucked him in, chewed him up and spat him out again. But you still can't let the bastards grind you down. Especially not at Christmas, when there's turkey to be eaten and the

Queen on telly and a few more drinks before a swift pint or two down The Railway. The landlady, Carol, is a fine woman, and sometimes gives him a drink on the house. He bets she will tonight. She has a glint in her eye, a spark you don't often see in women her age. She's bonny too, with a big chest adorned by shining gold chains. Always turned out well and always tanned, usually after having been off somewhere or other on holiday. It'd be a good life, he thinks, running a pub. Problem is he'd drink all the profits, but then again, it looks like Harry does that anyway. There's a lot of time, effort and money gone into that gut of his. He's happy with Lil, of course, but there's no harm in window shopping from time to time, and thank God he still has the energy to do it. There's a fella down The Venture who's had to go on Viagra, and he's only just past fifty. Frank has no worries on that score, Lil may not have the figure she used to but she's still got it where it counts and that's the main thing. There was that one time down The Railway at Christmas though when some joker had got some mistletoe out and Carol had held onto him for a bit longer than anyone else, her mouth pushing onto his a bit harder than he'd been expecting. He'd opened his eyes in surprise, but in the drunken merriment he'd kissed her back, given her behind an appreciative squeeze.

He combs his hair to the side in the bathroom, forcing his receding locks down with a dollop of Brylcreem. A splash of aftershave and his top button undone and he's ready to go. There's no worries that Lil will want to come along as she doesn't like The Railway.

'Are you sure you don't want to come for a quick one Lil?'

'No ta Frank, you go and have a good time, I'm going to watch telly for a bit longer. Bruce Forsyth's on a bit later and your mother's coming round.'

'Well, you know where I am if you change your mind.'

But she doesn't change her mind and Frank sinks a few in the company of Carol. She laughs at his jokes, whether they're funny or not, and he feels good to be away from the usual constraints for a while. No kids, no wife, no worries about redundancy, just beer and her heady perfume. The pub is pretty full, mainly with blokes who've come down to escape the family for a few hours like Frank has done. Frank begins to think Carol looks like his first childhood sweetheart would have done if she was standing there before him now. Andrea Wilde was her name and he'd been with her for a year or so before he met Lil. They eventually broke up because her father didn't approve. While not a teddy boy as such, Frank had had his rebellious ways. He drove a motorbike, he smoked, he'd quit school at fifteen. Andrea's father was a businessman and had warned Frank in no uncertain terms to stay away from his daughter or he'd be in serious trouble. He'd tried to meet her in secret afterwards, but she was scared of her father and didn't want to cross him. Then, almost immediately after that, he'd met Lil and they'd settled down. Jason was born soon after and Frank fell into line. The motorbike went, as did the greased-back hair, and he went off to work at Heinz, providing for his wife as more children came along.

Carol was a reminder in many ways of what could have happened. He could have run a pub, could have done anything really. He had loved Lil, and still did, but it was a love born out of familiarity and routine. He couldn't remember there being much of a spark even in the early days, they'd just sort of fallen in together as they were expected to. Back then you married young and had kids. Sometimes though, when he comes to places like this, he can remember another time, a different time in his life. He'd been young and daft and reckless, as all kids were, but every now and then he felt like he'd turned into a different person altogether. He never imagined it being like this. When he'd got the job and him and Lil had started out there'd been so many chances, so many opportunities. Kids came along and money was tight, but it was like an adventure, him and Lil were young and what you couldn't afford you didn't worry about and what you had you were happy with and grateful for. Heinz looked like it could be a good career move, set him up for life, he might even be able to retire early after a few promotions, move away to Spain or something. But he'd been passed over like he'd never been there, never mind that he'd been there nearly twenty years. As the drinks pile up his mood becomes even more bleak. There are some blokes in here with their wives, singing along to the karaoke, their arms around each other, a few even dancing away in front of the man singing *It's Now or Never.*

'You all right Frank love?' Carol says, leaning over the bar and giving him a good glimpse of her cleavage and a deep whiff of her perfume.

'Ay Carol love, champion.'

'You look like you could do with some cheering up. Harry's just popped out for a bit, why don't you come and have a brandy with me in the back room?'

Tomorrow will be too late.

Glass. Face. Blood. So much blood. It's spattered across his face and chest before the bouncers even pick him up and lift him out of the place. It's dripping down his shirt almost to his belt line when he's left fumbling around the street on his own, hardly able to see. He can feel people's hands on him, helping him along, girls screaming when they see him. Jason fights his way through the crowd in the pub, the ringside vantage points still packed. He feels someone grab his arm. It's Tony, Smithy's mate. 'Let me get you a drink Jay,' he says. 'You need to calm down.'

'Get off me Tony,' says Jason, not caring any more who he's pushing or where they land.

It's bedlam out in the street as well. Jason sees clowns and sailors and vampires all around him, as though he has just stumbled upon some bizarre carnival, but there is no sign of Johnny whatsoever. Jane walks by dressed as a medieval princess.

'Jane, have you seen Johnny?'

'He's been taken to the phone boxes, someone's calling an ambulance.'

Jason starts to run up King Street, trying to find a way through the hordes of people on the pavement and in the street. Music is everywhere, from the dance tunes on this side to the karaoke warblings across the road. For a minute none of this seems real, as though it is any other night out, no different. But tonight is Boxing Day night and Wigan is awash with drunken crowds. It is possibly the biggest social event of the year in town, the night when revellers don fancy dress and no one asks questions. No one wonders at drinking next to a policeman or Bart Simpson or the Village People. Jason had no idea how the whole thing got started, but it has been a tradition for as long as he or anyone he knows can remember. This year they are all dressed as pirates, fourteen of them, mixing the usual festivities with Dan's stag do, all of them wearing ripped jeans and bandanas, open shirts and eye patches, a plastic sword in each of their belts.

They'd spent the day on a pub crawl, starting off at the Bellingham and making their way along the line of pubs into town. Jason had been quietly impressed with Dan, they'd been drinking all day and unbeknownst to the stag, he'd been drinking three shots in every pint. However, somehow the poor lad had survived. A stripper arrived for them when they were in some beer garden or another, a young bird dressed as a policewoman. She'd walked in and mock arrested Dan before she started, the look of relief on his face when he finally realised it was a joke bringing cheers from all involved. They had dinner at the Moon Under Water, where Dan was made to eat spoonfuls of mustard and guacamole. A few concocted pints involving most of the optics on display, a shot of tequila here and there and the spiked drinks and he was understandably hammered, one of his work mates taking him home when his eyes rolled into the back of his head and the guacamole came back up onto the pavement. So the rest of them go to Bees Knees, where they down half-price pints and vodka chasers. Johnny's over talking to Supergirl at the bar and the next time Jason looks they're copping off. Then, out of the blue, some bird he knew at primary school comes over and latches herself onto his face and the competition is on. Nicola and Louise are out with other people tonight, they're all supposed to meet up later, in Chicago, but memories of when they were fifteen together come flooding back and any notions of responsibility or monogamy go hurtling out the window. It's three all by the time they reach King Street and go into the Ibiza bar.

It's only nine thirty and already everywhere is packed, queues for every pub, the street itself virtually pedestrianised as farm animals and Mexicans and nurses make their way from place to place. Down the stairs and then there's some more people they know. A few more beers and one more girl and Jason is having the night of his life. Then they see some bloke who Johnny owes money to. He's been avoiding him for months now, it's only forty quid, but it's forty quid Johnny wants in his own pocket, not someone else's. Smithy's a weasel but he's supposed to have connections. Nothing big though, so Johnny usually laughs the threats off. 'I'm just going the bog,' Jason says, leaving Johnny and Craig with the few remnants of the stag do, most of the others having wandered off in search of women, dancing up to likely girls on the dance floor. 'Don't worry, if he gives me any grief, he'll get it right back,' says Johnny.

The toilets are like another world. Just at the bottom of the steps there is an old fashioned sofa where some girls dressed in St Trinians' outfits are sitting and laughing, waving lacrosse sticks about. Jason smiles at them and then goes through the door to have a piss, undoing his fly and standing next to Ronald Reagan at the trough. He has no idea what is going on outside the toilets, in here everything is calm and jovial, people pissed up and in a festive mood. When he gets back upstairs there's a massive gap in the dance floor. It had been packed before he'd gone downstairs, but on his return it's like a circus, with people lining the outside instead of dancing in the middle. Jason pushes past Wallace and Gromit on his way up to the balcony and looks down. In the empty space where everyone used to be there are two lads fighting tooth and nail. Nice one, thinks Jason and steps onto his toes to get a better look. But then he sees the end of Johnny's shirt fly up in the middle of the ring and before he can move the place is chaos. He sees Johnny and Smithy getting lifted out of the bar and Johnny's face is covered in blood. Jason thinks at first that he's burst his nose, but the truth is much worse. By the phones he takes off his shirt to try and soak it up, but it's saturated in seconds. He takes his T-shirt off but it's still not enough. He looks around to try and see if he can spot Smithy, but the only people anywhere nearby are looking in horror and disbelief as Johnny drips onto the floor.

'I'm gonna kill that fucker, I'm gonna kill that fucker,' says Jason.

Johnny tries to say something and Jason sits next to him as he whispers, 'The first thing I thought was, Christ he's got a hard punch. I didn't realise it was a pint glass.'

The ambulance takes an age to turn up and by the time it does there's a pool of deep red on the pavement between Johnny's feet.

'Come on girls, we're going in here!'

Blackpool is buzzing. It's different to Wigan in so many ways. Denise misses the fancy dress round town, but not too much as they're all dressed up anyway. She has a big white veil draped over her head, while a learner driver's L-badge is stuck to the fairy wings on her back. She is bladdered, no doubt about it.

They'd spent the day at the Tower and been on The Big One at the Pleasure Beach, with no one allowed to bottle it. Halfway down the first drop Jenny had spewed the champagne they'd been drinking on the train all over the edge, everyone nearly choking as they got stuck between laughing and screaming as the bubbles came down her nose. Even walking along the seafront in the afternoon they'd attracted attention from blokes. They walked around the piers and along the promenade and men leered out of the trams at them, wolf whistles galore and shouts of encouragement mixed in with the drink.

It's a sunny day, but the wind blows a gale across from the Irish Sea so they pop into one of the amusement arcades over the road. Denise gets bored quickly, but she has to wait for some of the older ones who get gripped by the bandits the minute they're in there. She begins to regret asking her mum and certain older members of the Tesco work force when she eventually almost has to drag them out of the place so they can find a pub.

By late afternoon she's lost count of how much she's had. There are fifteen of them altogether and they've all been buying drinks for her, and that's not including how many blokes have plied her with rum and cokes when they come over from time to time. The greatest thing about being on a hen do is the power it gives them over men. Some of the braver ones come over to try and join in with the bawdiness, but once the drink has been bought for the bride they are soon surplus to requirements and either leave when ignored or when they are ridiculed into retreating back to the bar. Denise wonders how Dan's stag do is going and begins to worry herself as to whether or not he'll behave himself. She knows about the stripper his mates have hired and she begins to imagine what is going on back in Wigan, his face when she takes her clothes off, his mates and the way they are when women are around. The mob mentality of her friends is bad enough, never mind the boys when they get together. She's not been allowed a stripper as a few of the older women have said it's not the sort of thing they want to see. Fuck knows what they're even doing here some of them, sitting in the corner, sipping on Campari and sodas and making faces whenever one of the younger girls makes a lewd comment. Thank fuck most of them aren't coming to the club. Her mum is, but at least she knows how to have a good time.

They go to The Palace that night, and the girls mix time on the dance floor with vodka and Bacardi. They are all dressed as school girls, even her mum, which means pretty much all the male attention in the place is centred on them. Denise loses count of how many hands go underneath her skirt, and after a while she doesn't even bother to turn round and give the culprit a dirty look. Men grab her on the dance floor, arms circling her from behind, and she dances with some of them, her mum's laughter letting her know that she's not going too far. Lil's always wanted to dance around a handbag with the younger ones and so she places hers in the middle of the circle. She even gets a bit of attention herself, squealing with pleasure when a young lad's hands go on her hips and sway her about. She can't take it for too long though and heads off early with some of the others. Denise argues and tries to persuade her to stay, but underneath it all she is glad to be there just with her mates, able to get really into it and have a flirt and a lot more to drink. A song comes on that she's not too bothered about so she takes time off from dancing to have a drink at the bar and it is there where the trouble starts.

She'd been thinking about Dan, about how much she loves him and is looking forward to getting married. But with the drink inside her, her thoughts start to twist and she suddenly starts thinking of the future again. Only this time, the imagined future is one of several kids, of a baby-battered body, Dan's gut growing by the month as he loses the interest and the will to keep in shape. She is alone in their house, a grotty little shit hole in Ashton, waiting for the kids to fall asleep while Dan is off somewhere with his mates, something that happens more and more frequently these days. She hasn't had time to go to college after the first one came, her days and nights taken up with breast feeding and her nipples painful all the time. Dan supports them both but he spends so much time away from home, either at work or down the pub. She gets older and fatter and her dreams fade away into dust until she can barely remember feeling any different, as though it was always supposed to be this way. Denise has seen it happen, seen men and women with the life sucked out of them slowly, like a drip attached to their arm, draining the life force away, until their dreams and their young selves might as well be the figment of some romantic imagination. The next thing she knows she's crying. And the next hand that reaches under her skirt to give her a quick pinch is grabbed and welcomed.

They sit in a circle as the sun sets in the distance, still drinking from their bottles. They have decided to go into Wigan tonight, when it gets a bit later. Mark loves Boxing Day for the free rein it gives him over things, and this one even more than usual. Denise and her mum are in Blackpool, his dad is in The Railway, and Jason doesn't give a monkey's what he does anyway. For some reason the bloke in the off licence was being strict today so Jason bought his drink for him, a bottle of Merrydown and two cans of lager. They've been out drinking since just after three, although he's taking it slower than some of the others, knowing one or two might not even last through the evening. But he is intent on doing so. They are going into town as Reservoir Dogs, Mark using the suit he had to wear to his grandmother's funeral and some shades. It's the best way to get around underage drinking in the pubs, although there are certain ones that will serve them no matter what they wear. Jamie throws another can over his shoulder. He bought a six-pack but everyone knows he drinks less than half a can before throwing each one away. He does it because it makes him look like a big drinker, but they all know what's really going on. Jamie once told them all he'd drunk a bottle of Slazenger aftershave one day when he really needed a drink and there was no beer in the house. Mark actually hopes this is true, although he doubts it, as that would be true desperation to be cool.

There are bound to be loads of people he knows from school out tonight and he is especially hoping to bump into Sam. He's already snogged her, at the school Christmas disco, and she let him feel her up and finger her in the girls' toilets. It was nothing like the time in Alexandra Park when he'd been a bit wary and a bit unsure. His encounter with Sam had been amazing and, because the lights had been on at the time, he has a vivid memory to go over in his mind whenever he wants to. They had been drinking before the disco in the main hall and he'd been quite pissed, but he can still remember the way she had put her head back and moaned when his hand had gone up her skirt. He wants it to happen again and has tonight down as the big night. But when they get to Cheers later on, she is nowhere to be seen. Some of her mates are out, but she is not, although his enthusiasm is hard to dent with all the beer inside him and the come-on's he's getting from Sam's mate Cheryl. When it had got too dark to continue on the field they'd all gone back to his house, which was deserted as Jason was getting ready to go into town at Johnny's. They were going as pirates, and Mark was going as a Reservoir Dog. There were only five of them, but it meant they all got to choose their own names. Mark was Mr Brown. Jason had told him what pubs to go to, but he already knows to a certain extent, some people in his class have been going into town for over a year now, and Mark has been in twice before.

Cheers is best because they never ask how old you are. Because of this there is a peculiar mix of clientele within its garish multicoloured walls. While many of the drinkers are men who are near, if not past, retirement age, there are also groups that are obviously not even out of school yet. Mark has been in there both times he's been into town. Crossing the boundary between pavement and pub interior had been a big step and Mark had been a nervous wreck on his first attempt. He and Jamie had walked in and didn't realise how small it was so were nearly out the back door before the guy behind the bar said downstairs wasn't open yet. They made out like they knew what he was talking about and went back over to the bar, Mark ordering pints for them both and having to hide his grin when two full glasses were placed before him. But then two coppers had walked in not five minutes after them and started looking around. Mark, Jamie and the barman had just stood there, shaking, before the coppers finally turned and walked out again, bringing a sigh from the barman, while Mark and Jamie continued to drink with quivering hands. They didn't have any ID on them, some fake ones had been knocking around school, but Mark didn't have the five quid spare it took to buy one. Luckily they're both tall enough to pass for older and so most of the time they don't need it. You can't get into the better bars without ID, but Cheers is a great introduction to drinking round town when you're only fifteen. Karaoke is king in Cheers and Mark and his mates take the piss out of some of the singers, especially when Jamie does a drunken rendition of *Twist and Shout*. It gets him the necessary attention though and pretty soon he's copping off with some girl in the back room. Mark gets duped into singing *Daydream Believer* on his own when Dave says he'll sing it with him and then backs off at the last minute, leaving Mark embarrassed on stage alone. However, he receives a big cheer when he finishes, and it gets him talking to Cheryl again.

'So you missing Sam then?'

'Where is she tonight anyway?'

'She couldn't come out, her family have got this big thing on.'

'Oh right.'

'Do you fancy her?'

'She's all right.'

'She says you snogged her at the Christmas party.'

'Are you going to give us a song then?'

'Am I bollocks!'

'Why not? I bet you've got a great voice.'

'There is no way I'm getting up there and singing. No chance,' Cheryl says.

'Go on, you know you want to. I did it.'

'And you were good, that's why I'm not going up. I've got a terrible voice.'

'I bet you haven't. I bet you're really good. Why are you looking so down anyway? You can't be down, it's Boxing Day for God's sake.'

'Why don't you cheer me up then?'

He needed fifty-six stitches in the end. Fifty-six fucking stitches in his face. The police had been called in and although Smithy was possibly looking at a jail sentence and couldn't get anywhere near Jason or Johnny or face getting banged up for even longer, his mates can do what they like. Jason has heard stories about baseball bats and dark streets, about months in hospital and broken bones. It's New Year's Eve and even at work he can't relax. Working in the computer warehouse is the best thing he's ever done though. He's officially still only a junior but his boss reckons he'll send him on a fork lift driving course soon, get him trained up with the chance of better pay in the future. The sales team have exceeded next month's targets already and Jason gets called into the office. For once he isn't in there to receive a bollocking for being late or messing something up, but to get seventy quid in his hand in cash. He thinks about asking what it's for, but he knows better by now. If someone puts money in your hand you take it and don't ask questions, simple as that. There's going to be a big party at his house tonight and with the extra money he knows he can get even more shitfaced than usual. Nicola's coming too, and Johnny and Louise. It's a good job it's a house party as Johnny isn't exactly in the mood to go out on the town. Mind you, Jason doesn't feel like it either – it's not even a week since everything happened and what he saw in the hospital doesn't make him feel like celebrating much.

He always used to think in the past that if he got into trouble, a fight he couldn't win, he'd just shove a bottle in the person's face and run. He hadn't realised what the damage would be, the mess it made and the blood that inevitably came afterwards. He'd never seen so much in his life. When the ambulance arrived the paramedics had helped Johnny into the back and there'd been a trail of blood along the floor behind him. After a nurse had cleaned up Johnny's face in the hospital, Jason had come over to talk to him before they starting stitching him up, to offer a few words of encouragement. But Johnny had asked how bad it looked and Jason hadn't been able to answer him. It wasn't just how many cuts covered his face, but how deep they were and how close some of them ran next to his eye, his neck. The doctor said an inch either way and he'd either be blind or dead. If it's not one thing, it's another. He's finally got a job he likes, or at least one he can tolerate, a girlfriend he thinks he might be falling for, and then his best mate gets a pint glass in the face. How can you win? He tries not to think about it, filling a cardboard box carrying some computer parts with packing so it won't get crushed in the mail. He thinks instead to the night ahead, the party, the drinks, and Nicola. When his working day finally comes to an end, he picks up a hammer and heads out of the warehouse.

The hammer felt heavy in his jeans, uncomfortable and pushing against his hip. But he can't be too careful walking around these days, whether it's near his house or anywhere else, especially after what had been said and done. He'd sworn to get even with Smithy, to knock his fucking head in after what he had done to Johnny, and now he too was a hunted man. One wrong step around these parts, bump into the wrong people and you could be in trouble. If you came across a few of them it could be goodnight, they'd make sure you wouldn't be around for a few weeks to take any revenge. So he has to take a hammer with him everywhere. It was dark outside early these days, the sun went down well before he left work. He has a small collection of knives at home, but they'd be more trouble than they were worth. He couldn't get into a knife fight, anything could happen, and he's not even sure he could use one if it came down to it. But it was different with a hammer. Like that time when a group of lads from another school had come round for a big fight. It had nothing to do with him, he only vaguely knew the people who were involved and wasn't anywhere near when the feud had started, but he had somehow been swept up into it and become involved when he didn't need to. He'd stolen a G-clamp from the woodwork rooms and taken it down to the school gates, ready to take it out of his blazer at any time and start swinging should anything happen. Thankfully it hadn't that time, the lads from his school had shit one and gone home when they saw their welcoming party at the gates. Neither had it kicked off like he thought it would when he had cut down a rope swing in the woods, not realising that it belonged to one of the gangs near his house, and meaning he'd carried a hammer with him whenever he went out for three weeks afterwards. But this time was different. He could walk into any number of Smithy's mates at any time, they knew where he lived and could easily have found out where he was working. He had to be ready at all times, and he let out a sigh of relief when he reached his car unscathed.

Denise kisses Dan hello, hoping she is still managing to conceal the intense guilt she feels inside. She's heard the stories from his stag night, how he was in bed by midnight, how he'd drunk himself, or at least been forced into drinking himself, into a coma. And she remembered how the daylight had streamed in through the hotel window, had woken her up earlier than she wanted to, her hangover hitting her like a sledgehammer, opening her eyes and seeing the naked bloke in bed next to her. Why had she been so stupid? The other girls had laughed it off, had told her that was what she was supposed to do – her last night of freedom. But then most of them enjoyed last nights of freedom whenever they felt like it. She doesn't want to be like that. Dan was going to take care of her, she was in love with him and didn't want anyone else. Thank God her mum hadn't been in the club at the time and she'd had a chance to get back to the B&B before she woke up again. She hadn't noticed a thing and anything that was said afterwards was said out of her earshot. They all knew if she ever found out she'd skin them all alive, Denise for what she'd done, and the others for not stopping her. She'd been depressed and worried about the future and drunk, but it was still no excuse. He hadn't even been particularly good looking, just in the right place at the right time. She'd had her arse pinched throughout the night and told every previous offender to fuck off, but when this guy had put his hand under her skirt for a quick squeeze she'd turned on him like a cat on heat. She'd actually dragged him upstairs in the club, round to a bit where the balcony was closed off and there were enough dark corners so that no one would be able to see them. She had unhooked her bra, put his hand down her tights, and gone at it like she was never going to be touched ever again. She would have felt like a total slag even if she wasn't engaged, and if that wasn't bad enough, she was expecting Dan's child. He'd taken her back to his hotel and they'd fucked before she finally passed out. The next thing she knew the light was shining through the window and she could hear him snoring away next to her.

But she has to forget it if things are to be okay. She cannot think about it for fear her guilt will give her away, that she'll say something when she's drunk, that some little detail might pop out. She can't remember the guy's name, that's one good thing about it at least. She needn't worry about ever saying it when Dan is around, but she has to constantly remind herself of her new story, of how she left the club early with the girls to go and get a kebab, not that she jumped in the back of a taxi with someone else, so that when she is questioned about what happened she will only recount the truth he will want to hear. Dan says he can remember very little about his own night out. The last thing he recalls is him and the other lads in the Moon Under Water before everything goes blank. Denise has been told what happened though, and what happened to Johnny later, and is thankful that Dan was nowhere near when it had kicked off or it might be him and not Johnny with the blue lines of stitches all across his face. Dan stays in the front room with her dad and Jason, watching *Zulu* on telly, while she goes into the kitchen to help her mum and the other women butter the barm cakes for tonight. Like in Tesco's, she uses the mundane task of buttering bread to take her mind off what has happened, what she has done, how she has betrayed him again. And thankfully it works for a while.

She wishes she could have a drink. The blokes are drinking cans of lager in the other room and her mum is dishing out wine, but whenever she asks, she is refused. Her mum has told her that her hen do was the last time alcohol should pass her lips until the birth: 'You have to be responsible now. It won't do you or the baby any good.' The women crowd around her as though in worship of her fertility, cooing over her ever expanding stomach, asking if it kicks yet, if she's had any cravings. The only thing she craves for now is an erase and rewind button on the last few months, to take her life back a step and erase what happened in the flat, erase what happened in Blackpool, let her relive it again and do it differently. The one thing she is happy about is her pregnancy. She can't drink, she can't smoke as much as she'd like to, but she is happy that they are going to have a baby and that she is getting married. The wedding's in February, so it'll be cold, but it doesn't matter. There'll be no honeymoon either until the baby is born, but waiting doesn't bother her anymore, it is not the future she is ashamed of.

He is ready for tonight. Ready to see Stacey, checking and rechecking his shirt, his hair, putting more aftershave on before another long look in the mirror. Recent events have made him confident, the way he talks to Sam at school, Cheryl on Boxing Day, the events down the alley. Stacey might be back with her bloke, but right now he doesn't care. He is anxious to see her anyway, wondering what she will be wearing, how she will smell, and the kiss at the turn of midnight. Anything can happen at New Year's, he can hold her from behind in the conga line, he can kiss her when Big Ben strikes and no one can question him about it. He's going to take full advantage of this rare opportunity. He kissed her last year, briefly, but it was memorable. When he'd gone to the bathroom later he'd seen the big smudge of red lipstick on his face and he hadn't wanted to wash it off. Then the blissful moment when she'd held his face, tutting and wiping the mark away with a tissue. He can't wait for the drinking, the singing, all of it. New Year's is a great time to be alive, when convention goes out the window and everyone is happy for once. There'll be even more people than usual at the party this time too. His mum and dad have been throwing parties every year for as long as he can remember, and every year they get bigger and better. Jason's not allowing him to go to the pub with him and his mates beforehand, but they'll be back before midnight, and anyway, he always gets talkative when he's drinking, so it's not like he'll be alone.

He wonders what other girls besides Stacey will be there too. On Boxing Day Cheryl had said loads of girls fancied him at school. He couldn't believe this. He'd actually said 'Where the fuck have they been all my life?' and then panicked that it might look like he was being desperate or something. But she'd just thought he was joking and carried on kissing him. To be honest, the kiss and everything else faded into insignificance behind those words. Not one girl fancied him, not just Sam, not just Cheryl, but loads. That's what she'd said. He looked at himself in a different light when he was getting dressed in front of the mirror now, wondering what had made these girls fancy him, wondering which aspects of his looks were the most appealing and therefore needed accentuating, especially for tonight. Although he has always enjoyed New Year's in the past, he's often felt a bit out of it, too young to join in properly, and not even allowed to drink. It was all different now though. He was allowed to drink, he could talk to strangers when he'd been drinking without the fear they'd think he was a loser, and there were girls out there who fancied him. He just hopes they are coming to the party.

Downstairs the music is getting going in the front room. He'd watched the end of *Zulu* that afternoon, but he's seen that film so many times he feels like he could act in it. The telly is probably still on, with the video set to record any decent films and the sound turned down. It'll be on all night without the sound on, until ten to midnight of course, when they'll all drunkenly watch Clive James and wait for Big Ben to strike the New Year. Then the kissing, *Auld Lang Syne*, and the conga down the street after Uncle Steve brings some coal through the front door. God knows why they do that, and he always feels Uncle Steve misses out a bit, only coming in after the chimes, but he doesn't seem to mind, and he does get a big kiss and a cheer after ringing the bell. It's raining outside, but his dad reckons it's forecast clear for later on, not that it matters, rain couldn't dampen anyone's mood on a night like tonight.

Mark looks in the mirror again, moves his collar one way and then the other, tries his shirt buttoned up to the top, then missing the top two. He still can't decide if he's ready or not but the rising volume of voices downstairs and the amount of times the door-bell's rung means the party's hotting up. He checks his hair one last time and looks out over the road. Her light isn't on and he panics that she's already arrived until he sees her, her mum and dad and her bloke hurrying across the road, shielding themselves from the rain. He dives over his bed and down the stairs, finally seeing the multitude of people gathered there, avoiding one of his more affectionate aunties trying to kiss him and opening the door before the bell even rings. They look surprised at first, but he brings them in, hellos being echoed all round the room. He takes their coats one by one, staring directly into Stacey's eyes as she removes hers and trying not to look at her chest or her stomach. He takes the coats upstairs to his mum and dad's room and places them on top of all the others, leaving hers until last, holding it to his face and breathing in the perfume splashed all over it before falling onto the bed with it in his arms still. Man oh man, he is ready for tonight.

'What I'll never understand is why we have a bleeding Australian doing the New Year in this country.'

'He's been here so long he passes for English now. Like Rolf Harris.'

'He's never off the fucking telly either.'

'I remember *Jake the Peg*, me. And *Two Little Boys*.'

'Rolf Harris looks a lot better at his age than you lot will when you get there.'

'Bloody charming that. 'Ere, Lil, can we have some more cans out here?'

'You can if you get them yourself you lazy get.'

'Women's bloody lib, I'm not kidding. They've got some things to answer for.'

'Like Germaine Greer. She's Australian too,' says Mark.

'You what lad?'

Mark decides to leave it. Every time he tries to get into a conversation he puts his foot in it somehow or he says something so that everyone looks at him like he's got two heads. It's only an hour off midnight and his head's swirling. Every now and then he sneaks a glance at Stacey, but she's looking all loved up, wiping food from the side of her bloke's mouth or smiling at him when he gets her a drink. That smile. If any bird ever looks at him in the way she looks and smiles at her bloke he'll die a happy man. He goes into the kitchen to get some more to drink. Every year the party generally gets split up into two sections, the men discussing football or boxing and drinking beer in the front room, while the women dish out glasses overfull with spirits and talk about people on telly in the kitchen. Mark tries to make an effort in the lounge but decides he'd be better off moving to the kitchen from now on. He gets on with the women better half the time anyway, besides there's food in here too and he picks up a couple of vol-au-vents on his way in.

'You all right our Mark?'

'Yeh, ta mum.'

'Eh Lil, isn't he growing up to be a heartbreaker? You'll have the women eating out of your hand before you get much older Mark. How old is he now Lil?'

'He's sixteen this time Moira.'

'Fifteen eh? Can he have a drink Lil? Do you want a drink love? He can have whatever he wants, can't he Lil?'

'Can I have some vodka?'

'Course you can love, come with me and I'll make you one.'

There are no girls his age to speak of and the ones Jason's brought back with him from the pub are either too old or taken anyway. Bollocks to it then. He decides to get pissed.

He sees Tracy sitting by the kitchen worktop drinking beer from a bottle. She looks quite good tonight. Most of the time she wears totally unflattering clothes like jogging pants or baggy jumpers or T-shirts that don't fit and her hair's usually scraped back across her head so her eyes near enough squint. But tonight her hair's done in the customary Wigan flick, permed down to her shoulders at the back and sides and doused with so much hair-spray her fringe sticks up absolutely rigid at the front, immovable as concrete. He notices she's managed to lose quite a bit of weight since having her little boy. She doesn't look as spotty as usual either and she's got a pretty revealing top on that's red and only goes across one shoulder. He still wouldn't touch her with a barge pole though, he's heard the stories about Tracy. She's got three kids counting the new one, supposedly from three different blokes. She's only eighteen and doesn't work. Supposedly one of the dads is married too, that's why he doesn't want anything to do with her. Mark sees her from time to time, either walking down the street or in town, usually with one kid or another, sometimes all three, and always smoking. She's smoking now and he looks away when she blows a cloud in his direction. He takes the vodka and Coke Moira hands him and settles in to get rat arsed.

'D'you want a drink Nicola? You can have whatever you want love.'

'Oh ta, can I have a Bacardi, Moira?'

'Mum, will you get us a can?'

'You're as lazy as your dad you are Jason. Do you want one and all Johnny?'

'All reet our Mark? You pissed already?' says Jason.

'I'm getting there.'

'Good lad. Cheers Mum.'

'How are you then Johnny? You're looking a lot better already you know,' says Lil.

'The doctors say there'll be some scars but they should go after a bit.'

'Well I hope the animal that did it to you gets sent down.'

'Let's bloody hope so. If he doesn't I'm not responsible for what I'll do to him.'

'Now don't you go getting involved Jason. Two wrongs don't make a right, no matter what's happened. Let the police sort him out.'

The men are getting into the party mood in the front room. Denise comes downstairs from the toilet to see Dan laughing with the gathering throng, holding her drink. She takes it off him and gets a tangible feeling of warmth when he puts his arm around her and kisses her cheek. Just as with what happened at the flat, she is beginning to put recent events behind her now, winning the battle over her conscience and telling herself it isn't worth worrying about. At least she can't be pregnant again. She looks at him and imagines what he'll look like when they get married, all suited up and handsome. He might be a bit rough round the edges sometimes but he's all she needs. He'll be a great dad too, she can tell. She just hopes she can be a good mother. Whatever it takes she'll do it so the three of them will be happy. She won't go to Ibiza, whether he lets her or not. She won't go out on the piss with the single girls from work unless there are a few there who are taken as well. What happened in Blackpool has shaken her a bit, but she knows she can change, has to change, as it'll be more than worth it in the end. She hasn't kissed or slept with anyone else while she's been with Dan and the one blip is something she won't repeat again. Like the girls said, her last night of freedom, and that's exactly what it was. In some ways it was a good thing that it had happened, it reminded her that she was happy just with Dan. The other bloke was an awful kisser, his tongue pushing too hard and spit going everywhere. She only vaguely remembers sleeping with him, but it was nothing to write home about, she's sure of that. Too much mucking about and fumbling around and sweat. She always thought it wasn't worth the hassle and now she knows for sure.

'What you drinking Denise?'

'It's just orange juice Dad, don't worry.'

'You'll have to keep your eye on that one Dan. I'll tell you what though, I've paid enough out to keep her up till now, it's time some other bugger did.'

'Thanks a lot Dad.'

'I'm only messing love. You're the apple of my eye sweetheart and now you've got yourself a good bloke too. I'm happy for you both. When are you tying the knot then Jason? Does it not feel funny, your younger sister beating you to the altar?'

'It's fine by me. She's welcome to it.'

Jason gets a dig in the ribs for this from Nicola, but he can't help it, it's true. His sister getting married has made him think about a few things, like where he's going with Nicola for a start. He loves her and everything, but he can't stop thinking he's falling into a hole he won't be able to get out of. His mum used to tell him years ago that she didn't care what he did as long as she never had any irate fathers knocking down her door. Well, she might not have that with Nicola, but it was definitely getting serious. She'd even mentioned rings the other week, what sort she liked, how much you were supposed to spend on them and stuff, and constantly going on about how good Denise's wedding was going to be and what dress she wants to wear on her own wedding day. It was starting to drive him round the bend. It's not like he can see himself going off with anyone else, but the idea of being tied down to one person for the rest of his life isn't that appealing either. Take Boxing Day for example, he'd copped off with four birds that night, and had a fucking good laugh along the way. There'd be none of that if this carried on with Nicola the way it was doing. It's a frightening thought and no mistake.

'What you thinking about Jay? You look totally out of it.'

'You what Nic? Oh nowt. Do you want another drink?'

'Aye go on then.'

Mark passes Jason on his way out of the kitchen as he's heading for the bathroom. His brother looks down at him, but even though they brush past each other in the doorway he somehow manages to stare straight through him. He's back and forth from the bog by this point, drink always makes him need to go about every ten seconds. It's good in a way because it means if he's stuck talking to someone he doesn't want to or, what's happening with increasing regularity as everyone gets more and more hammered, being mothered by any number of the women in the kitchen, he can just excuse himself and go for a piss. It's a cracking party. He's sitting in a good spot to watch Stacey whenever he feels like it, although he has to admit that as the night has progressed he's become less inclined to look at her. All she's ever doing is getting kissed by her bloke or talking about the baby with his mum or any of the other women. And he's a bit worried that as he gets more pissed he'll just start staring and he doesn't want that to happen, he's pretty sure that's all he's doing anyway.

The bathroom door's closed when he gets upstairs, but the little engaged sign isn't pulled over so he walks in anyway. He hears the squeal before he sees anything, but when he looks up, there's Tracy, sitting down, having a piss. He hides his eyes and apologises, pulling the door to with his free hand. He'd been wondering where she'd got to actually, she's probably the person he's liked talking to the most tonight. She's not as bad as he thought she would be from what his mum has told him, and she looks quite pretty close up, a bit too much make-up, but otherwise not half bad. It's the lip liner that has drawn his attention the most. Her lips are painted pink but round the edges there is a darker shade of red drawn along the outline of her mouth. Every time he looks at her his eyes are drawn to her mouth and then inwards, her lips perpetually held slightly apart with just a glimpse of whiteness underneath. He hears the toilet flush and stands to one side in preparation of her exit. The door opens and his eyes are once again focused on her lips as she stands there looking at him.

'I'm sorry, I didn't realise anyone was in there.'

'Don't worry about it. It doesn't bother me.'

Five minutes to midnight and everyone is taking their places, gathering around the telly as the last few moments are counted down. Jason has been downing shots with Johnny for the last hour or so and he is feeling somewhere between merry and outright drunk. He has his arm around Nicola, all his previous thoughts and fears about his situation with her have been pretty much resolved after Johnny reminded him about seeing Lee Davenport on Boxing Day. He'd bumped into him in Bees Knees before all the trouble started, which wasn't surprising, he more often than not saw people out who he used to play football with when he was younger. But the incident with Lee had stuck in his head more than most and thinking back to it helped him formulate a course of action for the future. Lee had been a total hell-raiser, a lad well known for the amount of women he'd shagged and the amount of blokes he'd beaten up. And there he had been, telling Jason all about his golf handicap and his wife. He had even called her over and she shook his hand. They'd managed to get a babysitter for the night, her mum, who was having a quiet night and didn't mind looking after the little one while they went out and enjoyed themselves. Jason had stared at him in near disbelief, beginning to wonder who was free from the gravitational pull of long-term relationships, marriage and kids. If not this guy, then who? But then he saw how happy he was, how calm he was, how in control of his own life he looked. He was still out on the piss, but instead of entering the dog eat dog world of pulling on a dance floor or in a pub, he had a wife he loved to be with and go home with. And there are far worse girls Jason could be tied down to. Boxing Day might incur bad memories after what happened to Johnny, but all the girls beforehand had made it a good night in some ways. He'd nearly felt like a kid again, moving from one girl to the next, a quick snog and grope here, a few pints, and then another bird a few minutes later. But for once the idea starts to lose its appeal. Here he is, in his house, watching Big Ben with his arm around a girl who really cares about him. Suddenly, standing in his front room with her, the idea of no more going out on the piss, no more shagging other girls, no more freedom, doesn't scare him. If Lee Davenport can handle it, then he certainly can. However, right then and there, watching the minute hand click ominously towards the hour hand, he makes a pre-New Year resolution. He will do it one more time. He will sleep with one more girl and then he'll give himself up forever. He looks up and sees Denise heading up the stairs, rushing so she can get back in time for the big moment. Then his mum comes over, smiling and slurring her words.

'Where's your dad Jay?'

'I don't know, I haven't seen him in a bit.'

Frank doesn't know whether he's excited or shit scared as he and Carol roll about amongst the coats on his bed. It's risky, but the house is full and so Lil should be occupied somewhere or other. Stroke of genius asking her here on Boxing Day, absolute stroke of bloody genius. He's wanted his hands on those fabulous globes for as long as he can remember, and here he is, with well more than a handful to mess about with. While he kisses her he opens his eyes to look at his watch over her shoulder. They've got a couple of minutes before midnight and before anyone wonders where they are. He hears footsteps bounding up the stairs, but they don't sound like Lil's. He knows his wife's footsteps well enough by now. She's a fine woman is Carol, a woman with a full bosom and a hearty laugh. Her husband's downstairs and his wife's downstairs and none of them will be any the wiser. He hasn't felt this good since he was seventeen and could fumble around with girls with no strings attached whenever he found one that was willing enough. Carol is more than willing, that much is certain, she was the one who gave him the nod, and she was the one who was waiting for him in his bedroom when he got there. He'd closed the door behind him, well aware of the score, and they fell onto the bed like animals, with hungry mouths and clawing hands. But she stops him when he moves his hand around to her arse. He thinks maybe she's being a mock prude and so reaches down again, but this time she pulls away from him properly and turns to the door.

'What was that noise?'

'What noise? I didn't hear anything.'

'It sounded like the door being closed.'

'Don't be daft love, it was probably the bathroom. We'd better be getting back though, it's nearly midnight. I'll pop to the toilet and you head downstairs. I'll see you for another kiss later on.'

'You randy bugger. Here, wipe your face, I've got lipstick all over you.'

Mark was losing it at last. His virginity was being lost right this very moment, in his own room of all places, not down some shady alley or in a back street or a car or a field, but in his own bed, in his own house, on New Year's Eve. He was trying not to think about the significance of it all or it put him off what was actually happening. But he kept on thinking about it anyway, every in and out signifying his virginity slipping further and further away from him. Every minute that passed was a minute he was no longer a child. He was thinking how absurd the idea of losing your virginity was, it wasn't as though it was a wallet you could just drop somewhere, it took time and effort and it more slipped away than disappeared. He was worried about doing it wrong, about how much he'd had to drink. One thing he wasn't worried about was who he was doing it with. The girl next door fantasy he's had for so long was now a reality and thank goodness for it because half the time it was the only thing that was keeping him going.

They were both still partially dressed. She hadn't taken her top off, just slid it down as she had with her trousers which were now resting on his desk along with his Christmas revision. His trousers were dangling around his ankles and that put him off a bit, as did his shoes, which felt interminably heavy hanging off the end of the bed, but all in all he was just counting the seconds by that meant he was turning into a man.

He was slightly worried about time. He didn't know exactly how long this was supposed to last for. Was three minutes okay, ten minutes? It's only been a minute or so since they started and, while he's not about to come or anything, he does begin to wonder what sort of timescale he should be working towards. When he'd come out of the toilet she'd still been standing there. He had no idea what to do at first, but then she'd said it wasn't fair that he'd got a look at her and she hadn't seen him. His eyes hadn't moved from her mouth as the words formed: 'Which room's yours?' He'd pointed and she'd walked ahead of him, closing the door behind him and undoing his trousers. That bit hadn't taken long, so he was a little unsure of how long the actual act should take. Fuck it, he thought, I'll just keep moving until something happens.

Cheers rang out downstairs as Big Ben reached twelve chimes. Then came the doorbell and Uncle Steve with a lump of coal, heralding more cheers and spilled drinks. Everyone in the front room linked arms and formed two big circles for *Auld Lang Syne*, people stepping on furniture to all fit in. Half of them don't know the words, but the noise is enough, while those down in London sing away on the telly behind. Then the stereo is put back on, Black Lace cranked up to full blast, as they all form a line and dance out into the street. People come out of their houses and the street is filled, everyone shouting Happy New Year to everyone else and everyone kissing each other at least once.

Denise deflects questions about how she is when Dan asks, trying not to think about what she has just seen. Before she'd got to the toilet she'd heard noises coming from her mum and dad's room. She'd opened the door and there had been her dad and the woman from the pub up the road rolling about on the bed. She hadn't known what to do, what to say or think, and so had just mutely closed the door behind her again. Out in the street her dad comes over and tries to kiss her, she wants to avoid him altogether but just turns her cheek, not having the gall to completely blank him. She can smell the whisky on his breath, can smell the alcohol on everyone after having not touched a drop herself. She never realised it stank so much and especially on him when he comes near her. She remembers him calling her the apple of his eye earlier, and how good the words had made her feel. Now she looks at him in disgust as he links arms with her mum, dancing around with her as though nothing has just happened. But she cannot let it show, not now, not yet, and so she dances along with Dan and then Jason and Nicola and Johnny, not realising that Mark is missing.

He comes downstairs just in time for pie and peas. He's dying to say Happy New Year, but he knows everyone would think he was daft as it's well past midnight now. Well, he might have missed out on the actual minute, the dancing and singing, Big Ben and the revellers in Trafalgar Square, but at the end of the day he'd been shagging in his room. He feels purged, as though a huge weight has been lifted from him, and he goes over to one of the vodka bottles in the kitchen and pours himself a drink. His mother shoots him a look as though asking him what he's doing and he shoots one back that says, 'I am having some vodka. I am man enough to have vodka and that is what I am doing'. He drinks it in one as he's sobered up quite a bit after all the excitement upstairs and he wants to be back at the level he had been at before everything had happened. He tucks into the plate of pie and peas Moira hands him, not even looking up when Tracy leaves the house with her mum. She'd barely moved after he'd come, just waited for him to roll off her before standing up, adjusting her clothes and leaving. She'd said, 'See you around'. That was it. But for some unknown reason he didn't care. What did he want her to say? He'd been leading up to what had just happened his entire life but now it was over and that was all there was to it. He'd heard people talk about how the first time was always terrible, something to regret and with someone you regretted doing it with, but he has no such feelings. It had been really fucking good. Even the missed kiss from Stacey and the opportunity of grabbing her arse doesn't dwell on his mind. He heralds in the New Year with a grin full of meat, potato and sloppy wet peas.

Wedded Bliss

I never know where the time goes honestly I don't you can barely bring yourself to think before it's the end of the week and here we are with Christmas gone again and I don't even remember having a summer well that's half the problem when one day is much the same as the next there's no distinction when you don't get a proper summer I mean now we're past February and it's no different from September or even July if you think about it and it's not like we're even going to have a chance to get away from it all this year either not with our Denise and the baby on the way and the wedding just gone not that I mind though it's worth ten holidays on the Costa Brava to see your daughter getting married to such a nice lad he looked ever so handsome in his top hat and everything well they all did it was at St Matthews as you know oh it was a gorgeous ceremony and the vicar gave such a lovely sermon and even the rain held off long enough for all the photos to be taken I've never been so proud in all my life I was in floods I really was of course now they're waiting for the baby before they can get off on their honeymoon they've not booked anything like but Dan reckons he's going to give our Denise the surprise of her life I can't wait for them to go to be honest and have a chance to look after the little 'un and I can tell our Frank is as well it's the only thing keeping him going at the moment what with no definite job on the horizon still he's managed to get a bit of work here and there mind you but it's a vicious circle whenever he goes looking he gets turned down here and turned down there he's either got too much experience or not enough qualifications I don't know what they're looking for these days I really don't and he's taking it hard he's ever so down in the dumps especially when I come back from work I know they gave him a payout but I keep on telling him it won't last forever but he doesn't listen anymore just heads off to The Venture or the Labour club I've never seen him so broken before in my life I try and keep him motivated but it's like they took his life away sometimes when they took his job our Jason's trying to help out as much as possible but on his wage he can only do so much he's got his own life to think of and what with our Denise finishing work soon to have the baby she'll still get some maternity pay like but it won't be enough well it's never enough is it we've been dipping into our savings more and more and I know times are hard but it was supposed to be for when we retire I know I won't get much from the Hospice and Frank will only get out what he put in at Heinz and even that'll be a while in coming yet mind you I suppose we'll just have to keep on working until we've got enough to stop however long it takes at least Mark's stopped mithering me about going away to university though it finally looks like he's got his head sorted out or at least he doesn't talk about it as much anymore he's mentioned about getting a job over the summer before going to college but he has to get his results yet and if Frank isn't working I don't know how we'll be able to afford it saying that though we've been through tougher times than these and got through it have I shown you the wedding photos yet Jean they're fantastic the lot of them our Denise looks absolutely gorgeous and you can hardly see her bump I've still not sent a message to that shop to thank them for what they did but I'll be doing it soon as they did ever such a good job oh but she was ever so emotional I kept on having to tell her to smile as it's her wedding day she was just nervous probably and the do afterwards at The Beer Engine oh what a laugh we had the band were brilliant they really were playing sixties tunes and all sorts Dan's dad sorted that out apparently he knows some bloke or other who got it cheaper than usual it took me back I'm not joking it was like being sixteen again being thrown around that dance floor and Frank doing his speech I don't think I've seen him so happy in ages he was so proud and Nicola was there with our Jason I tell you I'm keeping my fingers crossed for a few wedding bells there an all it'd be brilliant to see him settled down as well he's been like a different person since he met her he thinks I don't know about him and what he gets up to but he can hardly fool his own mum that's why I'm glad he's met her she's such a lovely girl very polite and pretty and she manages to keep him on the straight and narrow better than I ever could hopefully he'll be getting a bit more money soon he's all set for this fork lift driving course his bosses are sending him on and that'll mean he's on a higher scale I hardly see him these days well he's either clocking up overtime or out drinking with the lads from the warehouse he still sees Johnny of course but I think what happened on Boxing Day shook the poor lad something chronic Jason says he doesn't want to go out round town until the court case has blown over that seems like it's taking forever and the thug who did it'll probably get away with a slap on the wrist I'll tell you I've no faith in the justice system anymore no faith at all when you read in the papers about drunk drivers killing people and all they get is six months it sickens you to think that things like that can happen mind you he looks a lot better than he did over New Year's well you saw him at the wedding he's still got the scars and everything but hopefully in time they'll fade away altogether our Denise still reckons she's going to take night classes when the baby's born but she'll have another thing coming I'll tell you she thinks having a child is just changing nappies and taking it for walks in the park but she'll learn soon enough not that I don't want for her to go and do what she wants I just know it won't be as easy as she seems to think at least she's got some sort of plan but Mark well I don't know what he wants to do these days he's going out more and more I try and tell him to stay in but he never listens he's getting as broody as Jason was at his age but then again I suppose if he can turn out like his brother he'll have done all right

'This is a bad idea you know.'

'Why?'

'You could get into trouble messing about with other people's wives, that's why. You've got Nicola for God's sake, why do you need anyone else?'

'I've told you about this before. I like Nicola a lot, I'm probably in love with her to tell the truth, but if I'm going to get tied down to someone I'm not going down without a fight.'

'Why can't you just leave it until your stag night – isn't that when you're supposed to have your last fling?'

'Since when did I ever do what I was supposed to do? Besides, I've done this before, it's piss easy.'

Jason scanned Mesnes Park for what he was looking for, a lone woman pushing a pram. He'd done this before, that was true enough, and it had worked too. He would have felt a bit more confident about it had it been summer, when girls discarded their inhibitions as fast as their clothes, but the dark clouds gathering above them could have their advantages too.

He and Johnny were sitting on the steps in front of the circular house that accommodates Fredericks cafe in the middle of the park. They'd walked through the front gates and along the wide main path, rubbing the statue's shoe on the way and making a wish as was tradition, a tradition which meant that while the weather had turned most of the seated figure green over the years, his right shoe had been polished to a stark contrasting gold. Jason knew what he had wished for, and that was one last fling with no strings attached. After seeing Denise getting married and how happy she and Dan had looked, he finally accepted that he wanted to marry Nicola. She had looked amazing on the day itself. It might have been overcast then too, but the sun had poked through the clouds from time to time and made her eyes sparkle, the bright blue highlighted spectacularly against her pale pink dress. He'd even imagined it had been their wedding day at one point and had been shocked to find that it didn't faze him in any way. She was the best looking girl he'd ever seen and he'd be lucky to have her. And if his sister could do it at three years younger than him, he didn't see why he couldn't.

So he'd have one last go on the merry-go-round to make sure he was ready. He had no intention of cheating when he was wed and he wanted to make sure he'd got it all out of his system before he tied the knot.

She'd be at work now in the town centre and he thought of her there, processing people's bank details behind the clear screen. He should be at work himself but he pulled a sicky to be with Johnny, who's been claiming since he got glassed. He was waiting for compensation and claiming for stress, which wasn't too far from the truth anyway. Since it happened Johnny has become much more edgy, nervous even, wherever they go, although especially in pubs. Jason had even noticed that he physically shuddered whenever anyone came near him with a pint glass. They'd been in the Pagefield the other week, standing getting served, when some old bloke had come to put his empty on the bar and Johnny had backed out of the way, his eyes fixed on the man's hands. This guy was nearly sixty but the sight of a glass too near scared the shit out of him. God knows how he was going to react at the trial, when he had to stand there and give evidence. Smithy had pleaded not guilty for some unfathomable reason and so Johnny had had to remember who was around when it had happened. Jason was secretly glad he hadn't been there, he didn't think he could stand up in a court and say anything, whether it helped Johnny or not. Fortunately there were already enough people coming forward to testify so he didn't have to feel guilty about his fears. It wasn't that he was afraid of Smithy, he'd even stopped carrying the hammer round with him now, it was the whole idea of going to court. If he could take him into a dark alley with a bat he'd know what to do, but to stand there in front of all those people, trying to think and talk straight, was somehow beyond his capabilities. Johnny's lawyer reckons Smithy could go down for three years for what he did, especially as Johnny could have died, and Jason hopes that happens: the cunt deserves everything he gets.

He pulled his jacket a little tighter around his chin as the wind picked up for a moment. Considering the sort of day it was, there were still a lot of people wandering about. Most were elderly people walking dogs or feeding the ducks, but every now and then there were a few birds, with big hoop earrings glinting and gold chains hanging half way down their shell suit tops. Too young most of them, but Jason eyes them up anyway. He knows what it'll take, a young mother with a pram, preferably married, with a dull fuck of a husband who pays her no attention as he's too busy turning his brain to mush in some factory. Any marks on their faces and it's a definite no-no, beaten wives are always the most faithful, not daring to do anything that might get them another crack.

He takes the beer can off Johnny and drinks deeply, it's got no fizz left and usually the warmth would make him shudder, but in this weather anything's a bonus. He always used to think that conventionally unhappy wives, the ones with real bastards for husbands, would be the easiest, that they'd be well up for some time away from someone who constantly beat them up; that they'd want to get them back the only way they feasibly could, but more often than not that wasn't the case. The ones who strayed were those who were seemingly best provided for, who had husbands that went out and earned money so they could stay home and look after the kids; who never hit them, didn't drink too much and were too tired to start an argument by the time they eventually got home. Poor bastards. He starts thinking maybe he should hit whoever he marries just to keep her in line, but he knows he couldn't do it even if he wanted to.

Suddenly he sees her, walking along behind a pram, coming straight down the path towards them. The walk up to the house always reminded Jason of *Rocky*. The path is wide and cracked, with bright flower beds on either side and the statue on your right. To get up to the building itself there are two flights of stone steps and if he thought about it properly they look nothing like the steps from the film, but Jason always had the music that played when Sylvester Stallone was running in his head whenever he walked up them. He and Johnny had slept rough in this very place one night a few years ago, drunkenly deciding to just stay out, to not bother going home. Fuck knows why, but it had been worth it, waking up early the next morning and watching the sun rising over the market building and the old grammar school. It had been freezing even though it had been the middle of summer, and when they woke up they'd nicked a couple of pints of milk from a nearby pub and then waited for McDonalds to open. At least it was better than sleeping in a bin the way Craig had done one time on his way home from town. He only lived about half a mile out but he hadn't even managed to make it that far. He'd been so drunk that he'd climbed into a big industrial bin by Morrisons before collapsing into his own piss in one of the corners.

Johnny looked across at Jason when he stood up. He'd seen the girl too and knew she was the one he was going to try for. He didn't understand why Jason wanted to do what he was doing, but he couldn't be bothered trying to talk him out of it anymore. Besides, he thought it was all a waste of time, he'd bomb out and then they'd spend God knows how long looking for another one until they decided to give up and go for a drink. Jason passed the can back to him and thought about what he was going to say. She was getting closer and he was making sure everything was set. She had a blue shell suit on with white trainers, not too old, but not too young either, decent looking in many ways. Blonde hair pulled back in a pony tail and no visible bruises to speak of. When he saw the ring on her left hand glint he gave Johnny a quick wink and followed her as she started towards the duck pond.

Denise stared at the ring on her finger, moving it around with her thumb as though making sure it was really real. She had always thought a ring would feel like a bind, an all encompassing wall around her, tying her down, blocking her in, but now she was happy with its connotations, the way she looked when she walked past a mirror and saw it shining, the way she felt to be a married woman, available to one man and one man alone. No need to ever go out on the pull again, putting on tight short clothes and parading around like some kind of peacock, trying to attract blokes who invariably turned out to be twats anyway. She had enjoyed her hen do in Blackpool, but she was glad she need never think about going to a place like The Palace again. Well, not in the way she had been doing since she was fourteen, all dressed up and looking for a bloke. She had grown tired of it ages ago and didn't regret she would never get the chance to do it ever again. She was Dan's wife now and she had a ring on her finger that she could flash at anyone who tried to stick their hand up her skirt. She still felt guilty for what she had done, but managed to absolve herself as she knew deep down that it had been the very last time. She had just been caught off guard, that was all. If that bloke had come up to her ten minutes later on, when she'd had time to think things through, get past the bad images she could see in her head, get past the awful feeling of sinking she'd had just at that moment, then nothing would have happened. Finally she felt as though she was floating, not sinking anymore.

It helped that she knew she didn't have long left at Tesco's. She elevated herself above those around her, her directionless workmates and the sheep wandering along the aisles. She had a purpose, a goal to aim for, and she wasn't worried by the thought of having to be patient to attain it. She was happy to wait, as, although it was frustrating in the short term, she knew it would all be worth it in the end. The baby would come and then they would go off on their honeymoon. The idea of time away from Wigan, just her and Dan, lazing around somewhere hot and sunny, was almost too much to bear and she had to stop herself from dwelling on the dream for too long. Instead she thought about what would happen when they came back, when they would look for a place to live, a place of their own, and, after a while, she would be settled enough to start her hairdressing courses, and even work in a salon for a while to gain experience.

Time at work no longer went by surely and steadily, it flew by, until the next thing she knew she was home again and having tea with her mum and dad and Mark. Jason finished work later and later these days, clocking up as much overtime as possible. The atmosphere between her mum and dad seemed a bit strained due to her dad still being out of work and they mostly stayed quiet, but Denise talked to Mark about school, about what books he was reading now and teasing him about what girls he fancied. Dan came round that evening and they stayed in her room watching telly together, her leaning back on his chest as he propped himself up against the headboard and tenderly stroked her stomach.

They still can't decide on names so she's taken another book from Tesco's after her mum threw the other one out by mistake. She's taken more and more things recently, gaining in confidence as her crimes continue to go undetected. Her room's a bit crowded since Dan moved some of his stuff in, but she doesn't mind, she's happy to make sacrifices as long as they don't have to live at his parents' house. The look Dan's mother had given her at the wedding had nearly cut her in two and she stayed well out of her way for most of the day. It hadn't rained at all, much to everyone's surprise, but the clouds hanging over Dan's mum's head were plain for her to see, even if no one else seemed to notice. She acted nice enough around her but Denise knew it was all an act, that his parents were far from happy that their son was getting married, and especially who to. They were stuck up bastards at the end of the day. They lived in Pemberton, but they had a bigger and newer house than most people and an elevated sense of self worth. It was a good job she wasn't allowed to drink as she's pretty sure a few home truths would have been aired if she'd had enough vodka and oranges. As it was the po-faced cow had just sat there and glowered at everyone, barely hiding her obvious contempt for the whole ceremony.

His dad had been good though, shaking hands with everyone and kissing her on the cheek – she'd even seen him drinking at the bar with her own dad later on, although she was pleased about this for Dan's sake, not her own. When her dad had given his speech she hadn't been able to even look at him. He hadn't acted any differently since New Year's Eve when he'd been messing about with another woman, so he obviously didn't know she'd seen him. She kept her head lowered as he heaped praise on her, saying what a wonderful daughter he was losing, glancing at her mum every now and then and wondering what to do. She still found it hard to describe the feeling of being the centre of attention, with everyone looking at her either with jealousy or admiration in their eyes. And when they had their first dance that night, she had never felt so special in all her life. His mother was fucked if she thought she was going to get anywhere near their child after the way she acted, but she was aching for it to come. If this was how happy married life was, just the two of them, she couldn't wait to start a family.

He hasn't spoken to Tracy since it happened, and for that he's grateful. He's seen her around town as usual, or in next door's back garden, but they haven't made any sort of contact, verbal or otherwise. Just days after it had happened he'd started worrying. I mean, this girl has had three different kids by three different men, she's obviously pretty fucking fertile. He hadn't used any protection, not even thinking to mention it, and as she hadn't, he presumed it was taken care of. When he thought about it properly though, he realised what an unbelievably stupid thing he'd done. The only saving grace is that she hasn't made any intimation that she is pregnant, or made any sort of effort to talk to him, so he presumes all is well and he's in the clear. However, that leaves another worrying thought in the back of his mind. If she's fertile enough to get knocked up by three different blokes (and possibly countless others, he has no doubt there is the chance she might just have got rid before) and if she isn't after he's slept with her, maybe he's infertile. He becomes obsessed with the idea that he's shooting blanks, just like the time he was convinced he had cancer after he had a shit once and it floated. He had stared into the bowl afterwards as it bobbed about and was positive there was some blood in there too. He'd spent weeks worrying about cancerous tumours growing inside him after reading a book in biology that said he had some of the symptoms, but when he'd gone to the doctors he'd near enough been laughed out of the surgery.

He certainly has the symptoms of sterility though. He's shagged a bird who gets pregnant every time a bloke looks at her in an alluring way and a few months down the line she was showing no signs of being up the duff at all. He's totally torn as to what to think. On the one hand, he doesn't want to have made her pregnant, on the other, he doesn't want to be infertile. He's dying to ask her if she had been on the pill or anything that night, but he can't bring himself to speak to her. He can't think of the right way he could put it and isn't sure if there would be a right way.

Things aren't too good at school either. Well, they're good in some ways and bad in others. No one believes him about Tracy but he doesn't care about that too much. He doesn't need approval or his mates to slap him on the back and say well done. He knows it's done and that's all that matters. His grades are still okay, although his teachers keep warning him he's going to have to start applying himself more if he's to live up to expectations in his exams. The bullying has shown no signs of resurfacing, but while he has achieved a new found sense of worth among the lads, he has been labelled a bastard by the girls. Sam found out about him and Cheryl on Boxing Day and went apeshit. It wasn't like he was going with her or anything at the time, but she barely speaks to him now, only looking across the yard every once in a while to give him daggers.

However, much to his surprise there is a silver lining even to this cloud. While there are some girls who look at him with distaste and even avoid him, he suddenly starts attracting attention from unexpected sources. Girls who previously wouldn't have looked at him twice start talking to him and, while his mini-reputation has ostracised him in some circles, conversely it makes him accepted in others. He starts smoking. A girl in his class called Alison stops him one day as he's on his way to the library and asks if he wants to go behind the science block for a cigarette. He's tried smoking a few times and never really liked it before, but Alison is not a girl you easily say no to. The uniform at school is brown and usually girls wear pleated brown skirts that start out thin at the waist and go out in a sort of triangle that covers the knee. White blouses are tucked in and ties worn long, all adding up to make a pretty unappealing ensemble. But there are some girls, and Alison is among them, who wear tight fitting skirts that end way above the knee, with blouses untucked and brown sweaters tied around the waist. The thin end of her tie barely reaches the fourth button on her blouse and denotes her status as someone who is cool. When he goes smoking with her he notices that all those gathered under the tree leaning against the science block wall have the same modifications to their uniforms. Alison finishes her cigarette, absently flicking the butt away with her nail, and, just before lighting another, undoes Mark's tie, rearranging it so that the fat end is tucked inside his shirt and only the thin end is visible, hanging down much shorter than usual. He untucks his shirt and leans against the science building, his throat burns a bit, but he carries on smoking regardless.

'Lovely day for a walk.'

'You what?'

'I said it's a lovely day for a walk.'

'Are you having a laugh? It's minging. Same as always.'

'Well, the sun's shining for a start.'

'Not much it's not. Suppose it makes a difference from all the fucking rain though.'

'Course it does. You're in trouble you know. You never rubbed the shoe when you were walking up the main path. I saw you. You have to rub the shoe when you come to this park.'

'Have you been watching me or summat? Rub what shoe?'

'On that statue when you walk in. You rub the right shoe, the one that's gold, and make a wish. They're supposed to come true every time if you do that.'

'You believe in that do you?'

'Why not? There's not much else to believe in these days, so you might as well try anything once.'

'I'll have to remember that.'

'You should, it's my own personal motto and it's never done me any harm. It yours, is it?'

'Yes. She's mine.'

'Little girl eh? She's a cracker, just like her mum.'

'What do you want?'

'Nothing. I just saw you walking and thought you might want some company. Do you come here often then?'

'That's bloody original. You'll have to try harder than that.'

'I don't mean it like that. I come down here every now and then, feed the ducks. It's nice round here when it's sunny.'

'She likes the ducks.'

'And what do you like?'

'Peace and quiet.'

'Don't be like that, it can get lonely wandering about on your own, you know. Besides, it looks like it could rain and I've got a coat you can borrow if it does.'

'What do you care?'

'I have a specific empathy with the single mother's plight.'

'Have you now?'

'I think young mothers give off a glow you just don't see in other women. It's very attractive all in all.'

'Is that right? And how young do you reckon I am?'

'I don't know, eighteen, nineteen.'

'I'm twenty-two. And I'm married.'

'That's not your fault is it? I can't be held responsible if your husband isn't looking after you.'

'He's twenty-five.'

'Good for him, I hope he does well.'

'Why are you talking to me?'

'Well, you can't help but spot a rose in a field of weeds can you?'

'Why aren't you at work?'

'Is that where your husband is?'

Denise had been a bit surprised and more than a bit embarrassed when her name had been called out over the Tannoy. Now she wishes that was all she felt. She'd been called to the main offices and told to sit outside. She played with her ring nervously while she waited, unsure of what was coming next. After a while they'd taken her into a room where three men had been sitting behind a table and then they'd hit her with it. They knew about her stealing. They had it on CCTV – her putting stuff into her bag at the side of her till. They were sacking her and she could count herself lucky they weren't going to press charges. They'd kept the stony looks on their faces even when she'd started crying uncontrollably. But what about her baby, she was expecting soon, she'd just got married, how could they afford for her to be sacked? But it turns out that's the main reason they aren't prosecuting and she should count herself lucky. She's hysterical by this point. Lucky? But it was only a few things, I'll pay for them, I'll bring them back. Then they bring up the small matter of her till, how it's been losing money recently, how the receipts don't add up. She feels shame pour down on her. They aren't angry, they're disappointed, they say, like what her mum used to say to her whenever she did anything naughty as a little kid. It's gross misconduct and they have to let her go. Don't make a scene, it's not what any of us want. So she goes back to her till, picks up her bag, then drops off her uniform, no one saying anything when some squeaky toy balls fall out of her coat and bounce under the table.

She lights a cigarette outside and walks towards town. She has no idea how she's going to tell her mum, her dad, Dan. The dole office is next to the bus station, so she pops in on her way home, sets up an appointment to sign on, at least deflecting the second of her mum's inevitable questions when she gets back. On the bus she stares out of the window at the scenery, the big Aldi outside town, the carpet shop where the old Unit Four cinema used to be, feeling once more as though things are passing her by. Inside she curses her stupidity at being caught. She thought she had been so careful to escape notice, but it turns out they were watching her every move. Harry, the good looking security guard who she said hello to every morning, had been put on special duty to watch her for the last three weeks after she was spotted putting something next to her till and when they checked at the end of her shift it had gone. She feels cheated. Nothing she took was of any value, and she had only ever taken five pounds from the till one time when she hadn't brought any money with her into work. But the till had been down for days, they said, and she begins to believe she was set up. She tells her mum this when she wonders why she's home early. The look on her face when she is told what has happened is one of disbelief and then anger. Denise begins to worry when her mum threatens to take action against the store, but she persuades her against it, saying if they have set her up, they can make sure they aren't found out.

Dan reacts in much the same way and she starts feeling guilty about lying, but the web is too far strung now to turn back. Her dad nearly hits the roof when he hears about it, but tea calms everyone down and reassurances that she will find another job abound. Dan tells her not to bother, he's set for a promotion soon and he wasn't all that happy about her working in her state anyway. So she starts to claim, turning up every two weeks to sign, swallowing her pride when she walks through the doors of the dole office – more than that in fact, she feels she has every right for what they did to her at Tesco's. The people down at the jobcentre try and encourage her back into work, but the offers are hardly appealing. Packing and picking at one place, cleaning offices here or there, wrapping frozen chickens. She goes to interviews anyway but is turned down by everyone due to the fact that she is beginning to get quite heavily pregnant. Her mum tells her she should do something about it, claim discrimination, but she doesn't want to. Instead, she wakes up late and sits in the living room on her own watching daytime telly, counting down the time, making the transition easily.

The Pier on a Wednesday night is where the malcontents gather; the place where disaffected teenagers go to express their individuality en masse. Long black clothes and make-up mingle with striped tights and tie-dye, combat jackets dance with low cut vests and Wonderbras. The Stone Roses and Charlatans mix with The Beatles and The Rolling Stones, Bob Dylan and Van Morrison, Nine Inch Nails and Rage against the Machine. Mark has never been here before but he is immediately taken in by the contrast of the dim lighting around the bar and the red and yellow flashing above the circular dance floor. On a weekend the place is packed with Scousers from Skem and Ormskirk, with dance music, sovereign rings and shell suits, but angst is the order of the day in mid-week, when goths and latter day mods mix in equal amounts. The canal is quiet outside, the lights from The Orwell pub over the water skim off its calm surface, while the pier itself protrudes undisturbed and nondescript on the opposite bank further up. But inside all is noise and dancing and music, cheap pints of snakebite and black and cider and warm bottles of beer while tangled couples roll around on sofas near the bar.

Mark walks around the outskirts of the dance floor looking for her. He knows that Sam comes here regularly on a Wednesday. He is quite conventionally dressed in trainers, jeans and a white T-shirt, but no one cares or notices once he is inside. Normal conventions do not exist within the drunken haziness of The Pier and those who are regarded as outsiders beyond the doors are allowed a rare moment of acceptance, equality and euphoria.

He's come with Alison and a few of her mates. His mates too, he supposes. They like the music, but there is the added bonus of the rebellious feeling of going out on a school night and also the entertainment involved in freak watching. Mark smiles to himself as he spots a circle of Liam Gallaghers on the dance floor, holding their beer bottles aloft and shaking them in time with the music. Since that first cigarette, Mark and Alison have become something of an item, bunking off together to go down to the disused railway line near school and get off with each other. They went round town on Saturday and she introduced him to the delights of shoplifting. They didn't take anything much, just a few packets of razor blades and some camera films, but it had been exhilarating nonetheless. Now she is showing him The Pier on a Wednesday and Mark is in his element, drinking pint after pint of sickly red snakebites and black and every now and then sitting at the tables in the back room upstairs. In the light, away from the music, a sub-section of the revellers gather to show their young pierced faces and tattoo-marked backs.

Mark stands on the balcony watching as a girl in a black cape dances slowly with an androgynous figure in front of her, long black hair hanging over a head held down, moving in time with the music. His mum is so wrapped up in Denise and the baby and the fact that she was sacked recently that she barely pays any attention to him and it is becoming increasingly easy to sneak out at night. His dad spends more and more time at the pub on a night too and Mark is afforded a sort of anonymity to come and go when he pleases.

He has learned how to forge his mum's signature so that any detention slips need never reach her. If she ever does wonder why he is late for his tea, he tells her he was studying round at one of his mates' houses. He hasn't seen Tracy about for a while either but he couldn't care less, he's decided he could just deny anything she had to say and probably be believed. And with Alison his sexual prowess is growing too. They've not been together long, but they've messed about quite a bit and he's pretty sure he'll get to shag her soon. He can't even remember the time when that prospect would have frightened him. He watches Alison on the dance floor with Kate, thinking how different things are for him now. A few months ago he wouldn't have thought he could have got anywhere near someone like her, but now it doesn't surprise him that he can. All the people he's out with are dotted around the club and when someone pats him on the shoulder he thinks they have come back to find him. He nearly takes a step back when he sees it is Sam.

'I've never seen you in here before,' she says drunkenly. He wonders if she would be talking to him if she was sober.

'First time for everything,' he says. 'Who are you out with?'

'Just a few mates. You?'

'Yeh, I've lost them all for a bit.'

'It's nice to see you anyway, I haven't really had a chance to talk to you in school.'

'You've been ignoring me you mean,' he says, for once feeling like he has power over her. At school she has had nothing to do with him and at first it had bothered him. Now he feels like he's on a different path and has no need for pleasantries.

'I know, I haven't meant to. It's just that I heard a few things about Boxing Day.'

'It's not like we were going out or anything Sam. Besides, I was wasted at the time.'

'Well, I'd like it if we could be friends again, that's all I wanted to say.'

Mark doesn't get a chance to reply as Alison arrives and grabs Sam by the arm, turning her around. 'What's going on here?' she says. Mark is just about to try and calm her down when she turns on Sam, shouting, 'Who the fuck do you think you're talking to, slag?' For some reason Mark's attention begins to drift away from what is going on in front of him. Everything suddenly becomes muted as another song starts up, and he's only half aware of Sam's reply that nothing was going on, they were just talking, before Alison spits in her face and then they're both on the floor, fighting. Mark looks down as Alison begins to get the upper hand, pushing Sam down and hitting her repeatedly in the face. Sam is trying to shield herself as the blows rain down on her upper body before Alison backs off, takes a two-step run up, and kicks her straight in the head. He hears Sam screaming, pleading for someone to stop her, but there is still time for another kick to hit its target before a bouncer grabs Alison from behind, picking her up and carrying her scrabbling towards the stairs. Kate grabs his arm, shouting at him to come on, they are leaving, and Mark manages one last look at Sam as she lies there sobbing, her face full of tear-streaked blood.

It's been a while since Jason has been in this situation, but, back in her house near the park, it feels as though it's not two minutes since he had that girl on the living room floor after an, up until that point, innocuous Friday night out. He's in another living room, but it's a younger home, not like the other time when there had been parents snoring away upstairs. He was surprised how easy this one had been – it mustn't be her first time and that turns him on even more.

Thank God for the English weather, the constant fucking rain. The minute the drops had started to fall she had walked back to her house with his coat over her head. She barely blinked when he followed her, didn't say anything when he walked in and put his arm around her from behind. The only time she did stop him was to push the pram into the kitchen and he followed her into the other room. Now she's on her knees between his legs and he sits back on the sofa, his eyes moving from the plates on the walls to her shell suit covered arse. The baby is crying in the other room and he doesn't give a fuck.

The one thing on his mind is Nicola and that perturbs him. It is reassuring in a way, but also annoying. Reassuring, as he knows he is doing the right thing by planning a future with her, and annoying because he starts seeing her face in the patterns on the decorative plates adorning the wall and that puts him off slightly. The girl between his legs is working wonders though. He looks down as her blonde head bobs up and down, her cheeks bulging whenever she pushes forward. He starts to feel as though he's in some kind of porn film, or like the Reader's Wives magazines he used to find in the woods. Somehow there had always been a conglomeration of torn up old porn magazines in the woods near his house. The thought that it was weird never crossed his mind, too happy in the find itself to worry about how they had got there or where they had come from. A girl was once raped in those woods, years and years ago, and the story had taken over the local news. He couldn't remember the exact details, but he had conjured up visions of a naked girl, tied up to a tree, in his head. How true this is to what actually happened he has no idea. He never imagined the woods to be dangerous before that, never thought about what porn magazines were doing there in the first place, or what kind of person would bring them in to read amongst the trees. But there were always ripped pages here and there and he and Johnny would meticulously brush away the dirt to reveal crumpled photographs of women with their legs spread, or of adverts for dirty phone lines, which more often than not were more explicit than the photo shoots themselves, showing women pulling their knickers down, leering up at the camera open mouthed with captions like 'Foul Mouthed Whore Wants To Make You Cum In Under Thirty Seconds' above them.

He manages to edge out the picture of Nicola from his mind by thinking back to the days spent with Johnny in the woods, collecting the countless scraps, painstakingly putting them together to try and make complete pages. He looks down to see the girl staring at him like they did in those old photos and he reaches behind her back to undo her bra. It's a nice house, the one that they're in. A nice family home, no doubt put together combining his money with the time she inevitably has on her hands in the day to make it look good. They've not said a word since coming back to the house, all the talking was done in the park. He'd tested the water with a conspiratorial look here, a well-timed double entendre there, and she'd responded in kind. He looks at her hand as it holds him, the wedding ring glinting up at him. Then he pushes her back onto the cream rug behind her and pulls down her shell suit bottoms. She has a good figure all in all. Nothing much to report up top, but enough, and a slim waist, which impresses him all the more after having a kid. That was the main thing that turned him on, that she'd regained her figure since giving birth, and he is confident Nicola will do the same. Mind you, he can't imagine this girl has ever had much meat on her.

He slips off her knickers and bears down, her mouth quick to return his kiss, her body obviously having been untouched for some time. He has just gone inside her, she has just moaned as he pushes down, when she suddenly freezes, as does he. She looks anxiously up at the ceiling, her nails digging into his back, and he looks over his shoulder as it becomes apparent that the noise they have both just heard was indeed the front door.

'Who the fuck is that?' he whispers as blind panic grips him from his head to his bare arse. But he already knows, even before she pushes him off and says, 'Who do you think it is? It's my fucking husband.'

He has never moved so fast in his life. Not even as a ten year old, well before drinking and smoking had slowed his body down, could he have pulled his trousers up and started looking for a way out as quickly as after she said it was her husband coming into the house. Why didn't she put the latch on the fucking door? He tries to work out which way to run. The sinking feeling really sets in when he realises the house is a back-to-back.

He feels as though he's working beneath himself, but what can he do? The baby is due any day now and after Denise got sacked someone had to keep the money coming in. Carol's out of the picture now and so a kid will be a welcome addition to his life, something to look forward to. She told him she couldn't carry on, that it was deceitful, but not before he admitted he'd leave Lil for her, which he now realises wasn't much of an offer. With Harry she's got the pub, and money coming in, and holidays whenever she wants. What can he offer her? He's sunk so low he's working in a factory off Enfield Street, only temporary, sweeping the floor and moving bits of plastic from one end of a line to another. But it brings in the money, or at least some money, and that helps ease the feeling of degradation inside him. No holiday again this year, but even that isn't so bad, all that ever happens is you go away somewhere where they don't cook the food right and it's so hot you just sit around all day sweating. You're on the bog more often than not and they don't even have water you can drink out the tap. At least he never slept with Carol, at least they never went that far. He doesn't feel as guilty as he would have done if it had gone further than a bit of a kiss and a cuddle. The only thing he really regrets is that he can't go to The Railway anymore, but then again, most of the time he only went because of her.

After what happened at New Year's he was pretty sure it was going to carry on, but she'd called a halt to the proceedings not long after. He hasn't seen her in nearly three months, but that's the way it goes sometimes. Easy come, easy go. Just like the jobs he's been doing since being made redundant. He's worked here and there, but it never amounts to much in the end. He finally did get a bit of work at Haydock, on the racecourse itself, although it was just picking up litter. He'd managed to make a bit of money on the side when a few bets came in, but one time he'd blown a whole day's pay on the final race, something he had to keep well hidden when he got home. Lil trusted him to put his money into their account so she never checked. He did worry what would happen if she ever did check, what she'd say if she found out. Then again, that was why he worried, he knew what she'd say, she'd hit the bloody roof, but what can she expect, working for just above minimum wage? Not only was it embarrassing, an affront to his pride, but it was nowhere near enough to pay the bills, so he had to gamble. He didn't put much down and every now and then they came through. He just needed a break, that was all, just needed one hot tip and they'd be sorted. For a while anyway.

At least they were better off than some. He'd met Dave from next door in the Labour club one night and he'd told him all about his Tracy, how she was pregnant yet again. He said he'd have to keep her locked up if it carried on like this. She's already got three kids and no support from a bloke. She gets money from the social, but this is the last straw. Once again they have no idea who the father is. They ask her over and over, but she won't tell them. She only bloody wants to keep it as well. For once, talking to Dave, Frank felt quite content with his home life. Denise might have a baby on the way herself, but at least she was married to a good bloke. He hadn't seen Jason's girlfriend around for a while, but he presumed he was still with her, and even Mark had pulled his finger out of his arse and was talking about getting a job over the summer. He still wanted to go to college mind, but if he was paying his own way Frank decided he could hardly argue – besides, he was learning all about the advantages of an education first hand for himself. No qualifications these days mean you don't get too far when looking for work. Thank God he didn't have a daughter like Tracy though, knocked up four times in nearly as many years, probably by as many different blokes. Sex is a time bomb round these parts. If you don't get some girl up the spout, you end up catching something that turns your dick into a burning, pus-filled mess. Dave had said he wasn't going to put up with it any longer, that she'd have to leave, get a council flat or something. He couldn't take having another kid about. He said he'd marched her down to the jobcentre and put the wheels in motion to get her into one of them flats in Scholes, or a house down Norley Hall or Worsley Mesnes. It didn't bloody matter where if the truth be known, just as long as she moved out and took her kids with her.

Frank leans against his broom and wipes his brow. The factory is boiling hot, the machines noisy all around, and he has gravelly dirt covering his hands and face. He's jolted back into action when he sees the supervisor coming. No matter what happens, you can't be seen slacking off for one single minute. It doesn't make a difference whether there's work to do or not, you have to look like you're doing something or they'll dock your pay or get rid of you altogether. He's had this job for a few days now and is hoping to keep it until the end of the week at least. There's nothing like enough work for him to do, but he isn't going to let them know that. He's far from fond of being ordered around by people either younger than him or by old fat blokes who love seeing him in this position, love their few hours of power over another human being. But he manages to cheer himself up ever so slightly by imagining himself as a young Arthur Seaton again, under the cosh, fighting back against the system from the bottom rung. He pushes the broom around, waiting for dinnertime so he can scan the paper for a likely bet that afternoon. It's all for the money, when all's said and done. He has enough in his pocket for a gamble and a drink when his shift finishes, and that's what matters in the end.

Denise felt the contractions early in the morning. Dan was asleep next to her, and while she didn't want to wake him up, she could definitely feel something happening. She got out of bed as slowly as she could and went to knock on her mum's door.

'Don't worry love,' her mum said, her eyes finding their focus almost immediately when Denise told her what was happening. 'It'll be a while yet. Go and put the kettle on love, I'll run you a bath.'

Thank God her mum was there to help. If she was on her own she'd be panicking by now, visions of births from TV programmes and films filling her head, screaming and sweating and rushing, phoning an ambulance straight away and getting to the hospital as soon as possible. But when her mum found out how far apart the contractions were and how strong they felt, she said it would take hours yet, that she should relax, she had plenty of time to get ready.

'No reason to wake anyone yet love. Go and make some tea.'

Denise put tea bags into two mugs and waited for the water to boil. She couldn't believe it was really happening, that by the end of the day she'd be a mother as well as a wife. She stirred in the milk and switched on the telly, hearing the water running upstairs. It was too early for her to be able to manage an actual programme, not that anything was on anyway, so she watched the pages on Ceefax, the ones they put on themselves, not the ones you actually choose. It was on World News but Denise paid little attention, the piano music sending her to sleep as her mind managed to float away from what was happening to her.

It doesn't stay like that for long though. Her mum comes downstairs and wakes her up, gets her to drink her tea and then sends her upstairs for a bath. The heat of the water doesn't allow Denise to fall back to sleep and she wonders if it's a good idea, having it as hot as it is. She has heard the stories about boiling baths and gin bottles and the last thing she wants to do is lose the baby after everything she and Dan have been through. And now the day has finally arrived. She looks down on her glistening stomach, rubbing water carefully around her extended navel. Another contraction comes, a little one, and she marvels that there is a little person inside her trying to get out. She wonders who it will look like most, her or Dan, trying not to think about the ordeal she will go through at some point later on. She's watched loads of videos about women giving birth and the pain frightens her. But the looks on the faces of the mother and father afterwards, and then the baby itself, make her know it will all be worth it. A new life is just about to start, not just for the baby, but for her and Dan as well. She'll give birth and then they'll go away for a while, just the two of them, away from this house which seems to get more crowded by the day. She and Dan are going to get a place as soon as he's saved enough money. She has a bit stashed away herself, not a lot, but once she can get back to work it won't take long for them to set out on their own.

Mark is shitting himself and no mistake. It's all he can think about. Forget exams, he can barely pick up a pen to write he's sweating so much. She's pregnant. He's seen her. He's seen her with that telltale bulge, propping her back up as she wheels the other ones around. He still hasn't spoken to her, but he'd have no idea what to say even if he could somehow find his voice from the recesses it has sunk to in his stomach. He can't believe it's true, but there it is, for all to see. Five months down the line, five months after he slept with her, and she's showing. It was ages before Denise got much of a stomach, but Tracy is in full bloom. He even begins to wish he was infertile, even that had to be better than this. How the hell was he supposed to tell his mum? How the hell was he supposed to tell anyone? His studies would have to stop, that's for sure. He'd have to get a job and support her or something. How can he have been so stupid? He stares at the exam paper before him, it's not even a real one and he still can't answer the questions. They're preparing for the real ones, they are so close now, but even with no pressure on him whatsoever he can't concentrate to save his life. He looks at the equations on the paper in his hands but they float away into the distance, long lines of numbers and letters stretching out to the horizon, the desk in front of him spinning downwards as though he's got vertigo. And that's exactly what it is. He's put himself on the edge of a cliff and now he's looking down into oblivion. His hand shoots up to be dismissed and he rushes out of the classroom, positive he's about to throw up.

He stares into the toilet bowl and the smell makes him feel sick, but nothing comes out. His life is flashing before his eyes and when he flushes the toilet, it's like he can hear it draining away. He washes his face and looks at himself in the cracked mirror. He only turned sixteen last month but he looks older already, old before his time, like so many fuck-ups he sees around town, their lives prematurely over, no hope to cling to, every day like all the others, pushing you one step closer to death.

Back in the classroom he looks at the paper again and feels sure he used to know how to answer the questions.

It's not like he even has to worry about Alison anymore. She buggered off with someone else a while back, a twenty year old with an Escort XR3i and an earring. He wasn't bothered, he was thankful in a way. He'd shagged her enough times to feel confident in what he was doing and pulling on a Friday has become a regular occurrence. He sees Sam around school every now and then and feels like he should say something, apologise for what happened maybe, but he doesn't. At the end of the day it's got nothing to do with him.

He spends most of his spare time down at the wreck of the old mill, drinking with the others, bottles of cider interspersed with whisky and sherry. The mum of one of the lads there owns an off licence and he nicks what he can, selling full bottles on for a fiver. A few swigs and you're totally fucked. He never finished *Lord of the Flies*, not having much time to read anymore, too busy at one park or another. He had a black eye the other week when some lad from another estate took exception to who he was getting off with and butted him. Mark turned and ran and when he was far enough away, sat and giggled by himself on the platform at Pemberton, the train tracks spinning in front of him.

Suddenly his teacher calls him over to her desk to speak to him, but the only word he can hear is baby. He can feel the sweat building up on the back of his neck. What does she mean, baby?

It's only been five months, it's not been long enough for God's sake, he's not ready for this, he's not ready. Then he hears his brother's and sister's names amongst the sounds coming from her mouth and he makes his way through the rain to the steps at the front of the school, grateful to get into Jason's car, grateful to get away from there.

Jason got the phone call at work. Up until that point it had been a normal day. It had been quiet at home when he left but he was too tired to wonder why. He'd just started to pack out the mail when Darren, his boss, had come over to tell him his mum was on the phone. And, with smiles and a few pats on the back, Jason was allowed to leave early to be with his family while his sister gave birth. Truth be told he didn't really want to go. He always thought she'd give birth in the middle of the night or something and he'd go and visit her afterwards. Why the hell did he have to be there? It was all his mum's idea of course, wanting the family together when the newest member arrived. He could hardly say he'd rather be at work, but he could think of better things to do than wait around a hospital with sick people wandering about all over the place. However, he'd been told in no uncertain terms that he had to go, so he was in his car, driving to Billinge where the maternity hospital was. He had to admit he'd been slightly excited and caught up in the moment when he'd told the others in the warehouse and Darren had said of course he could go early. The lads had sent him off with wishes of good luck and a sense of anticipation that it was an important event, but now he just felt numb. He tried phoning Nicola before he left, but the people at her work told him she'd gone on her dinner hour. 'At two o'clock?' he'd asked. They said she'd had a busy day and couldn't get out any earlier. It was like that all the time at the moment though. He hadn't seen her in nearly a week, something that had been unheard of up until now. They'd seen each other if not every day, then every other day, since they started going out, and now all of a sudden she wasn't taking his calls. He spoke to her briefly a couple of days ago when she'd answered the phone herself, but she said she couldn't see him, she had family problems to deal with. He said he'd go round and help her, keep her company, give her someone to talk to, but she said she didn't think it was a good idea.

He had no idea what was wrong with her. As far as he was concerned he was going to pop the question this summer. It was over a month since the incident in the house near the park and he was now well and truly convinced he didn't want anyone else. He thought that if he had visions of Nicola when he was with someone else then she was the one he really wanted to be with. Besides, he felt lucky to have escaped without injury or repercussions and what had happened had been more terrifying than exciting. When he'd heard the door opening he'd been on the verge of having a coronary as it was, and his accelerating heart rate was far from calmed when he caught a quick glimpse of the man mountain coming into the house. Her husband was a big bastard, tall and wide, but when Jason had been looking for a non-existent back door in the kitchen, he'd gone into the living room. While he was shouting at his wife and booming threats at whoever the hell was in his house, Jason had realised there was a clean line down the hallway and out the front door again. Thank God he'd left it open. If he'd had any brains at all he could have locked it and that would have meant Jason's only escape route would have been to jump out of one of the upstairs windows. Fuck that. He saw his opportunity and took it, sprinting as fast as he could for the door, holding his coat and T-shirt in one hand and his shoes in the other. The man mountain had appeared in the living room doorway a fraction too late to stop him and the adrenaline coursing through Jason's bloodstream meant he managed to shrug off the meaty fingers that grabbed at him. Once out of the house he had carried on running to the park, hiding behind the small building just inside the front gates and hurriedly putting the rest of his clothes back on. When he was satisfied he wasn't being followed, and his breathing pattern had returned to somewhere near normal, he made his way across the park and out the other side, heading for the Pagefield. He phoned Johnny on his mobile and they met up for a pint. Jason was smiling again and when Johnny rebuked him for being so stupid, he said he didn't care, what was the point of life if you weren't going to live it? Besides, that was the last time, he was going on the straight and narrow from now on. He was at last ready to settle down with Nicola and be happy, although he didn't tell Johnny, he wanted to surprise him by asking him to be his best man.

However, that was all a bit null and void if he couldn't even bloody speak to her. God knows what was up with her, maybe she was on the blob or something. In that case he'd better steer clear anyway, but she'd always said she wanted to be with him when Denise gave birth, and now it had worked out that he could be there in the hospital, he was gutted she couldn't come too. He tried her mobile a few times but it was engaged, so he sent her a text message to phone him as soon as she could. He picked up Mark from school and they headed to the hospital together. He noticed Mark looked out of sorts but didn't say anything at first. When he looked again he saw his brother's face was nearly white.

'What the bloody hell's wrong with you?'

'Nothing.'

'Not so bad, you look like a bloody ghost. There's nothing to be scared of you know, it's not like they'll let you see anything. We're just there to give support to our Denise, that's all. Besides, it'll be good for Mum. They won't let you in the delivery room if that's what you're looking so peaky about, this isn't a biology lesson you know. We'll just stand around for God knows how long getting bored out of our arses. You should hear Mum though, she's excited as hell about it. I could barely get her off the phone when she called me.'

In the hospital the screaming had long stopped. Mark never thought he'd be allowed so near to Denise, that he'd be in the corridor just outside while everything happened. He felt weird being there with his mum and dad and Jason and Dan, all together, waiting for the baby to come. Lil was flapping about, nervous as anything, but excited too, she could hardly sit down.

Frank kept nipping off to the coffee machine, his hands fidgety around the sides of the plastic cups, his knees twitching, and he kept standing up even though Lil told him to sit down. Jason was trying to phone Nicola but every time he came back with the same reply, she wasn't there. Mark had thought being here would have bothered him, that all he'd be able to think about was Tracy and her being pregnant, but now all he cared about was whether Denise and the baby were okay.

Nurses and doctors came and went throughout the whole thing and when the double doors opened for brief moments Mark could hear Denise making all sorts of weird noises. Dan had finally come round but he'd not been allowed back into the delivery room since he'd fainted. It had all been a bit farcical. His unconscious body was pulled out of the delivery room by a male nurse and then someone rubbed smelling salts under his nose until he woke up again. Lil wasn't allowed in either, she was too squeamish, and Mark felt a bit sorry for Denise going through it on her own, although she said that's what she wanted.

They all sat in silence afterwards, a tense silence, with everyone looking at each other and not knowing what to do. Then the doors opened again as the midwife came out. Mark could hear the baby crying faintly inside. The midwife was smiling as she said, 'It's a boy!' Dan's face lit up and he looked like he would start crying himself. Lil hugged him, tears streaking mascara all down her face. She'd been there all the way through and was tired out.

'Go on then lad,' she said. 'Go and see her.' Dan walked slowly to the delivery room, stepping past the midwife, whose face dropped as he went through the doors.

'Is he the father?'

'Aye,' said Lil, 'he'll make a grand dad.'

Mark was smiling to himself and Jason came over grinning, putting one hand on Mark's shoulder and patting him on the back with the other. Frank went over and kissed Lil and for the first time in a long time Mark felt like there was some real feeling of family between them all. Lil and Frank put their arms around Mark and Jason, crushing their boys to them, Lil shaking as she sobbed out loud. It nearly brought tears to his own eyes, the idea that they were all together to witness his sister giving birth to another addition to the family. For a few blissful moments Mark felt fantastic. Then all hell broke loose.

All he could hear was shouting from behind the closed doors to the delivery room. Mark was the first to break away from the hug and look to where the noise was coming from. Something was wrong but he couldn't tell what and so he just looked at his mum and dad, unsure of what to say. The midwife who'd come out with the news was looking a bit awkward. She went over to the doors, which swung open just as she reached them and sent her flying back into the corridor, crashing against the far wall with blood pouring from her nose onto the greasy-clean floor. Mark stepped forward to help her when she cried out, but stopped when he saw Dan in the doorway, his face red as fire, veins popping out on his neck, screaming back into the room, 'You fucking hooer! You fucking hooer!'

'What is it?' said Lil. 'What's wrong?' But there was no stopping the bedlam. Jason went over to try and grab Dan's arm, but Dan shook him off.

'You fucking, fucking hooer!' he spat, slamming the door back again, not even noticing the midwife as she tried to pick herself up from the slippery mess she was making on the floor. 'What's going on?' said Mark, following Dan as he stormed off down the corridor. He didn't catch what Dan said at first as his words were slurring in anger. Then he heard:

'It's black.'

'What?' Mark said.

'Your fucking sister has had a fucking coon baby,' he said. Mark stopped dead in his tracks and watched Dan crash through the double doors in front of him before kicking a bin over and disappearing around the corner.

'Did I just hear that right?' said Jason, who had come up to stand next to Mark. He was grinning again, but it was a reaction born out of nervousness more than anything else.

Frank didn't take kindly to it though. 'What the fuck are you smiling about?' he shouted, before heading over to the delivery room saying, 'Jesus Christ, what's she done?'

Lil's tears had changed from those of joy to confusion and Mark realised no one had gone over to help the midwife so he went to her and picked her up off the floor. She seemed in shock and walked off down the corridor, blood dripping onto the front of her uniform.

'I'll go after Dan,' Jason said and sprinted off.

Mark just stood there, not knowing what the hell he could do. There was movement everywhere. More shouting, from Frank this time, and more crying from Denise, came from the delivery room whenever the doors swung open as more people arrived and left. Someone asked Mark where the midwife had gone and he pointed blankly down the corridor. Frank was bundled out of the delivery room, still shouting at Denise long after the doors had closed.

'I don't fucking believe this,' he said before walking off. Lil shot Mark a quick glance and went after him.

Mark was rooted to the spot, feeling completely hollow. He could hear his sister sobbing away as people continued to pass by, but he couldn't bring himself to go in and see her, reassure her, do something at least. He felt like he was standing in a glass box, able to see everything, but unable to interact or move. He couldn't cry like his mum and he couldn't get angry like his dad and Dan. When the pandemonium finally died down and only he remained in the corridor, he walked back the way they had come in and sat on a wall underneath the main entrance porch. There was no one in the car park and he couldn't see Jason or Dan or his mum or his dad. It was absolutely chucking it down outside, sheets of water falling so fast that puddles like miniature lakes formed immediately and rivers started flowing down the street as the drains were suddenly overloaded. Lightning flashed and thunder cracked, the sound breaking right beside him as it echoed off the houses across the road, while streetlamps began to illuminate hours earlier than they should - one of those days when the sky is so dark you wonder if the rain will ever stop.

Walking Away

The rain falls heavy on Enfield Street, the clouds dark and sombre above, the terraced red brick glistening. Jason walks along, alone, hands in pockets, head held down, his neck getting wet. It's Friday night but he's not sure what he's going to do.

She said she doesn't want to see him again. She told him it was over. It wouldn't be so bad if she'd given him a reason, but she just said they can't go out anymore.

'Is there someone else?'

'No.'

'Have I done something wrong?'

'Just go. Just go.'

For once in his life he'd found someone he could be happy with and she's the one to pull the plug. It's so ironic it makes him sick. He's turned girls down in the past, given them the shove off, not feeling a reason was necessary, not really caring what they thought. He doesn't understand.

'There's nothing to understand, it's over, that's all.'

And that is all.

He hasn't seen her since. It's been three weeks and he still can't stop thinking about her. He hadn't been able to find Dan when he'd left the hospital so he'd gone into town instead to see her, meet her from work. He should have known there was something wrong when she wouldn't return his phone calls, but he was certain there was when her face dropped the minute she saw him. He gave her a lift home, telling her about everything that had happened, but she hadn't looked like she'd cared even then. And when he'd pushed her for an answer as to what was wrong she'd told him. It felt like he'd been shot.

Two days before his sister had given birth he'd been happy as Larry. He'd checked his bank balance and he'd saved enough to be able to spend his next month's wages on a ring. He could blow the lot, get something special. His mum told him that was what you were supposed to do, her face beaming at the idea that he was going to get married as well, on top of how good she felt about Denise having a baby. He'd never seen her so happy. She'd even hugged him, said how proud she was that they were all growing up so well. Now the whole thing was in ruins, Denise's baby, her marriage, and Nicola. If there was ever one time in his life he felt like he should cry, this was it. But he still couldn't. He'd ring Johnny, see what he was up to. They hadn't seen each other for a bit either. Jason had kept a low profile in the house since the birth, all that ever seemed to go on was arguments and screaming and crying, so he usually went off to be on his own somewhere, unable to face being in anyone else's company. Everything had changed in such a short space of time he couldn't believe it. Everything had gone wrong and it didn't look as though it would ever be right again.

In his home life there had pretty much only ever been one thing that remained constant – teatime. Specific days heralded specific foods and everyone was supposed to gather at as near to the same time as they could manage. Mondays were fish fingers and beans, Tuesdays meant burger and chips, Wednesday was pizza, Thursday cottage pie, Friday chicken and chips, Saturday was a free for all, while Sunday was always roast beef. The line up had hardly changed for years and the usual clink of someone knocking their glass into the person's sitting next to them, or the clatter of knives and forks on plates, made sure there was always a level of noise even when conversation was at a minimum. Not any more though. Everyone kept out of each other's way at the dinner table, not wanting to touch, no one saying a word for fear of breaking the quiet.

It seemed like Denise hadn't stopped crying since it happened. She just lay locked in her room, hardly ever coming out, the new baby being fed by their mum. Jason looked at it, not knowing who to feel sorry for, the baby or his sister. It wasn't its fault, what had happened, but it would bear the brunt of the aftermath, that was for sure. And Dan, it wasn't his fault either, and since the birth he spent almost all of his time at his parents' house. He came back every now and then and that was when the arguments would start, people screaming at each other, pots breaking, the lot.

Denise swore blind she hadn't slept with anyone else, but the protests fell on disbelieving ears as there was no other explanation for what she had brought into the world. Jason didn't want to get involved and as soon as he finished his tea he stood from the table and went out the front door again, not answering his mum when she called after him, not even bothering to take a shower or a bath, just wanting to get away. He called Johnny from The Venture when his willpower to be alone began to fade. After all, it was a Friday night. The pub was filling up slowly. It wasn't a raucous place like The Railway, it was more posh, an old man's or family pub. But while Jason wanted to drink, he also wanted to be away from noise, and this was the place to come. The only sounds were the clacking of pool balls from the next room, the faint hint of a television with its sound turned down, and the fruit machine. He took his pint into the far room, which had an old style fire and big wooden tables, and sat down, lighting a cigarette. Tearing up beer mats, he tried to look on the bright side of things. It was the weekend, he and Johnny were probably going to get out of their brains on beer, even if it was in a quiet pub, and he didn't need to blow a month's pay on a ring anymore. He thought over the advantages of the single life again and again, thinking of all the girls he knew he could call up and see, maybe even go round to their houses and get lucky, but only the smile he showed Johnny when he arrived was real.

She has felt as though she wanted to be someone else her whole life, and never more so than right now. All her fears have been realised, everything that could have gone wrong has done. She's read about post-natal depression and wonders if that is why she feels like she does. But she is sure that doesn't even begin to describe the things going through her head. She has the memory of a morning after, waking up in a strange room with her knickers down past her knees, dried up flakes between her legs, and now she has a baby. It would have been bad enough, awful, terrible, horrifying, but she's married and that makes it a million times worse. She thinks back to when she found out, the fears she had then, the idea of a hospital bed and some pills. Retrospect is a dreadful thing when you eventually become aware of the consequences of your actions. She could have got rid of it and no one would have been any the wiser. Now she has no job, no husband, a baby from a night she can't remember. The only option she has to get out of this is to tell people what happened, but even then she cannot be sure she will be believed.

Why did she not say anything before? Why did she leave it until now? Why did she allow Dan to think that he was the father when he couldn't have been? She doesn't even know if she can use the word 'rape' as she can't remember anything. Surely they would believe her though, how could they not? She is not a liar, she wouldn't make something like this up. The truth was the only way out now, that she must have conceived when she had been unconscious, or at least too pissed to know what was happening. But what will they think of her then? Maybe it will be even worse.

She can hear her child crying downstairs and that sets her off again. She never would have thought it possible that one person could cry so much. And while it may not be Dan's, it is hers. It is her own flesh and blood and to get rid of it would be monstrous. But she must be a monster because she wants nothing to do with it. It has destroyed her life, brought all her dreams crashing down around her. She should be on her honeymoon with Dan right now. They would have caught a plane earlier in the week and at this moment she should be on a beach drinking cocktails or fucking in the sea. Instead she is face down on her bed, wearing her dressing gown, surrounded by pillows and covers that she puts over her head whenever she hears the baby making noises downstairs. She has already decided to put it up for adoption, give it to some family that can't have kids. She cannot cope with it, cannot bring it up herself. But if she does tell people what happened, what then? She will have to admit to being so out of her brains at a party that she had sex with someone else, or was forced to have sex by someone else, but she has no idea who. And then the search for whoever it was, going round to John's flat, asking questions. John despises the police, has been in trouble before, would possibly come after her if she kicked up a fuss about that night in his flat. She considers just telling Dan what happened, but he doesn't want to see her, never mind speak to her.

The relief when they finally pulled the baby from her was incredible, despite her body being wracked and tired, her head light after all the pain. But when she looked up to see it the relief was replaced by fear. It was dark. It had black hair and an Asian face. It was not white like her or Dan and when he came in and saw it too she thought he was going to explode. She was a whore. All she remembers is crying, looking at Dan as his eyes burned into her, wanting somehow to explain, but the words were lost somewhere far down in her throat and she couldn't bring herself to speak. He was screaming at her, calling her names, his anger flooding down onto her. And then he was gone. She'd looked up when the door had opened again, hoping it was him, hoping there was something she could say, some way to erase this awful mistake, some words she could use to change the way he had looked at her, but it was her dad and the look on his face was even worse. It wasn't just anger, it was true hatred. Hatred for her, not for whoever it was at the party, not for what had happened to her. He didn't know, no one knew. And what made it even more painful was that she didn't know either. She didn't know whether to hate the person or herself for what had happened. She could have said anything, done anything. She could have looked at this person with passion in her eyes, could have pulled him on top of her, could have fought off his complaints and said she really did want to do this, no she wasn't too drunk, take me, take me now.

It could have been anyone. Admittedly there were certain things that had to be true. For a start the person had to be Asian. The baby was Asian. She did not know any Asian people apart from Tariq, but he had not been at the party. So whoever it was had been a stranger up until that night. She refused to believe that she had welcomed a stranger into her willingly, not knowing who they were. It didn't matter how out of it she had been, she didn't believe she was capable of that. The last thing she remembers is wondering where Dan was. Where had he been? She hadn't even asked him the next day, but she was sure he hadn't been in the flat when she left that morning. Whoever it was must have taken advantage of her, known she was alone, known she was drunk and stoned, and gone through with it just the same. And now everyone hated her for it. She doesn't care what the consequences will be, she cannot allow what is happening to her to be her fault. So she will tell them. She will tell them all. She will tell everyone everything that happened, that she had been drunk, that she can't remember anything other than waking up the next morning with her underwear around her knees. And then God help her after that.

Do I wake or sleep? Mark tries to concentrate, saying the words inside his head in the hope that they will connect to something, but the effort is ultimately in vain. He flicks through the book on the desk in front of him, trying to focus, trying not to look around to see how everyone else in the hall is coping for fear that he will see them all scribbling away, writing answers to questions he is monumentally failing to grasp. He can hear a hundred pens on paper, feverishly writing, but he cannot bring himself to touch the whiteness of his own exam paper. No words or explanations for what he is reading are coming to mind. He has been sitting there for a full half hour, his eyes searching the verse, but nothing is clicking in his head, no memory of what he has been told in class comes back to him. *A drowsy numbness pains my sense.* He can understand that well enough. It is as though a veil has been cast over his mind and his memory. He remembers sitting in class, listening to the teacher talking about Keats, writing notes in his book, confident he was grasping what he was being told. Now, sitting there in the main assembly hall, he feels absolutely alone, even though there are hundreds like him all going through the same thing. All he knows is how important his exams are and what will happen if he does not do well, the wasted time he will have spent, the wasted time he will be forced to spend if something does not come to him soon.

Blind panic has not set in yet, but it is on the way. This is his last exam, his English literature exam, and after the mess he made of all the others, history, French, science, maths, he thought this one might be his one saving grace. He wonders if dyslexia has suddenly descended on him, that it is not his fault, but his brain that is failing him in a way he cannot prevent. His eyes move from the book to the antiquated desk he is sitting at, reading the graffiti written there by students in the past, who, like him, could not cope with the task at hand and wrote things on the grotty wood instead. *To do is to be – Descartes. To be is to do – Sartre. Do be do be do – Sinatra.* He nearly manages a smile when he reads this until he looks again at the poetry book. You're supposed to spend an hour on the poetry bit, fifteen minutes preparing an answer and then forty-five minutes writing. Two questions, one on poetry, one on prose. One and three-quarter hours in all. But already the clock is ticking towards his first forty-five minutes and he has not written a thing. He doesn't even dare to look at *Lord of the Flies.* He never finished it, does not know what happens at the end. He remembers his teacher saying something about innocence being lost, but he has no idea how to write about what he doesn't know. Then he starts panicking that he isn't paying attention, that his mind should stay on poetry for now, he should write something, anything.

But all he can think about is Tracy and her expanding stomach. Every day that passes she is a day nearer to giving birth, a day further away from New Year's Eve. He even tried talking to her recently, but he couldn't get his legs to move when he considered walking after her down the street. He tried focusing on his school work, ploughing through it one last time, but it was as though he'd never studied anything written in his books. Scientific and mathematical equations look like a foreign language to him and in his aural French test he had barely understood a word being spoken on the tape. It is as though the last five years of his life have just suddenly melted away into void. He was set to get A's in most of his subjects, but now he is uncertain whether he will even pass or not.

Fade far away, dissolve, and quite forget. It's as though all the lines were written for him. If only he could write an essay on himself, how the poem might as well be about him, about Tracy, the baby, his life slipping through his fingers like sand, but the questions don't make sense. He doesn't know how to connect the poet with his surroundings, cannot understand the use of nature or the poet's transference of emotion. He doesn't know what any of it means. *O, for a draught of vintage!* But all he can picture is vintage Merrydown, the gold and silver labels, last Friday night when he had gone out instead of studying, rolled around on an embankment with some girl whose name he couldn't remember because he was so pissed.

He can remember the hospital, how he had sat outside as the rain came down and the thunder cracked, counting the breaks between lightning and noise until the storm started to fade away. He can remember New Year's Eve, how Tracy had taken him into his room, how they hadn't fully undressed, just exposed the bits that needed to touch. He can remember seeing her the other day, how she had looked at him as he stared at her bump, how she looked away when his eyes had moved from her stomach to her face before he realised she was looking back at him. How he had known in that second, before she turned away, that she was pregnant by him, that his life was over, that he was going to be a father. But he cannot remember what his teacher had said to him when they were reading Keats, what themes they should focus on in the exam, which lines best represented the different aspects of his poetry. He looked up at the clock to see he had been in the room, writing nothing, for well over an hour. Then he looked down at the paper to see the blankness before him. Picking up the pen at his side he wrote *I cannot see what flowers are at my feet* before standing and walking out of the hall.

'Nic, let me in, we need to talk! Nicola, talk to me please. I know why you're being like this, but I can explain. It's not what you think.' Jason knocked on the front door again before banging the side of his fist against the wood. He'd been at her house for nearly twenty minutes and he knew she was in, but it was becoming increasingly obvious that she had no intention of opening the door. He considered just walking away, but he couldn't, he wanted to be with her and he wanted her to know how he felt. But she didn't want anything to do with him anymore, she had made that much clear. Johnny had told her what happened in the park, had told her all about him going back to that girl's house. Everything Jason had told him in the Pagefield that day Johnny had recounted back to Nicola and now she wouldn't see him, said she never wanted to see or speak to him ever again.

Jason looked up at her window, trying to see if there was some form of movement from inside, a curtain twitching, anything. She had told him he could go to hell, like his slag of a sister. But he wanted her anyway. He hadn't seen Johnny since the previous Friday night in The Venture, when they had been talking as usual until Johnny's stark revelation. He hadn't even seemed like he cared that he had betrayed him, that he had ruined his future. He just told him, then and there, what he had done, matter of factly, as though it was supposed to happen, that he was in the right and Jason had no cause for complaint.

'I don't understand why she won't see me,' Jason said, staring into his beer.

'I told her about what you did. In the park.'

'You did fucking what?'

'She knew anyway Jay. She knew you cheated on her. You gave her something didn't you? You gave her an STD.'

Jason's stomach sank with the news, but he remained adamant it was not his fault. 'But that wasn't it! I barely touched that girl, her husband came back – I told you.'

'Yeh, you told me, and I didn't think it was right,' said Johnny, refusing to return Jason's deadly stare.

'I don't give a flying fuck what you thought – what the fuck had it got to do with you? It was none of your fucking business!'

'Yes it was my business. She asked me if you'd been with anyone else and I told her. She told me about having something and I didn't want to lie to her.'

'When did you talk to her? What have you been saying behind my back? You're supposed to be my mate for Christ's sake – what the fuck were you thinking?' Jason couldn't believe what he was hearing. Most of all he couldn't believe how Johnny was acting, as though all they were talking about was the weather.

'Keep your voice down will you, you're shouting,' said Johnny, his eyes still fixed on the table. 'She came to my house one night and we talked. She was upset. I didn't think it was fair on her.'

'What the hell was she doing at your house?'

'She was upset.'

'Jesus Christ, did you fuck her?'

'Calm down will you? No I didn't. Of course I didn't. We just talked,' said Johnny, briefly glancing up at Jason. It was the first time their eyes had met since the conversation had started and in that momentary contact Jason suddenly understood why Johnny had done this to him.

'But you wanted to. I know what this is. You didn't think it was fair that she fancied me, that's what this is. You couldn't bear to see me with her, that's it, isn't it? You jealous fucking prick, you've screwed everything up.'

'You screwed everything up. You don't deserve a bird like her,' Johnny's tone began to turn from one of disapproval to outright dislike.

'I don't believe what I'm hearing, I really don't. You just couldn't keep your mouth shut for ten fucking minutes.'

'I don't care what you say, I know I did the right thing.'

'Right thing for who? I wanted to fucking marry her and now you've fucked it up big time. She's not happy and I'm not happy, so tell me, who did you do this for? For yourself you selfish bastard.' They were both drinking at speed now, Jason consuming his beer between each time he spoke, needing something to do with his hands so that he didn't smack Johnny in the face.

'Selfish? Take a look at yourself Jay. Mates don't put each other in situations they don't want to be in. You knew I didn't think it was right and you did it anyway.'

'It had nothing to do with you. Mates don't mess around with each other's lives. You deserved that glass in your face that night. I don't fucking blame him for doing it. I feel like fucking doing it myself right now.' He did, but he was sorry for saying it aloud. At that moment he knew he would never see Johnny again.

'You cunt. I can't believe you just said that.'

'Fuck you, you traitorous get. You've fucked my life up,' said Jason, standing up and walking away. He couldn't believe his anger had gone so far, but there was no turning back now. Johnny called after him, not caring his final remarks were being addressed to Jason's back.

'You can do that all by yourself Jay. You don't need any help from me. You're a waster and always fucking will be.'

Jason knew he had to leave when he did as the desire to hit Johnny began to scare him. Johnny'd had the stitches out of his face and although the scars were still there, the stitching wasn't and his face looked like a target. But despite everything, he knew he couldn't have actually done it. They'd known each other since they were six years old. Jason had once sat talking to a girl at school years ago when she had seen some bloke she said she had been good friends with in the past, before adding they weren't friends anymore and that she hadn't seen him for ages. Jason hadn't understood how that could happen at the time. He believed that real friendships were forever, that he would know the same people from childhood until he was dead. Now he knew it didn't work like that. He was unlikely to see Johnny again and it didn't look like he would ever see Nicola again. Suddenly, thinking about it all, he did get angry. He'd been angry at Johnny in the pub, but impotent too. He didn't have the energy to lash out, to fight him, and so he had just walked away. Now he wanted to hurt him. It was Saturday afternoon and Johnny would be working. There had always been something between him and Louise that he hadn't been able to define, always a bit too much flirtation, a touch that lasted a bit too long. Now he planned to make it last even longer.

Jason felt sure that when Louise met Johnny for the first time she had wanted to be with him really. But he didn't want to know because she had a kid so Johnny had started going out with her instead. After taking one last look up at Nicola's window he set off in the direction of Louise's house, to talk to her, to tell her about the problems he and Johnny were having, that he and Nicola had finished, that he was free again. A few drinks and anything could happen.

When he arrived he stood outside and smoothed his hair down, formulating a method of attack in his head. He couldn't believe what had happened to him and Johnny, he never really wanted Nicola anyway, you're looking very fine today Lou. But just as he was about to knock on the front door he noticed the curtains were closed. The curtains were never closed in the day, not even when she was watching telly, as the sun didn't shine on the front of her house. He went over to the window and could hear sounds coming from inside. Through a chink in the curtain he saw her, lying on her back, with someone on top of her. He thought at first it was Johnny, that he must have the day off or something, but then he saw this person had an earring in his right ear. Johnny never wore jewellery, apart from a gold chain with half a heart, with Louise owning the other half. It wasn't Johnny at all, but it was definitely Louise, getting shagged on the living room floor by some bloke Jason didn't know. Two weeks ago

Jason would have banged on the front door and gone in to smash the guy's face in, but he didn't have the strength or the inclination anymore. Instead he turned to walk away, wishing he could feel some sense of triumph, but not feeling anything.

she's not been down to bingo for I don't know how long you know well I'm not surprised after what's been happening and after all her haughtiness about Tracy over the road being pregnant as well and her going on and on about the wedding a penny bloody wedding at that in all her finery and pomp and it turned out black as the ace of spades I'll tell you it took all I had to stop myself from laughing I mean I'm not one who wants to benefit from someone else's misfortune but the way she used to talk about it how she was better than everyone else because she had a ring on her finger and how Jason's got this new job and how good it is for him and how much he likes it and their Mark going off to university to make something of himself all the time making out like our Ryan working at McDonalds is some sort of failure it serves her bloody right I don't know who she thinks she is Lady bloody Muck honestly and as if that wasn't bad enough of course now they're going round telling people she was raped that she went to some party and someone must have taken advantage of her the cheek of it the absolute bloody nerve it makes you sick it really does what levels people will stoop to I was only reading the other week of that girl in the paper about how she'd had too much to drink one night and nine months later there's a baby to show for it well I mean don't get me wrong rape's a terrible thing when it happens but these days it's gone too far the other way a girl does something she regrets after drinking God knows how much and immediately claims it wasn't her fault of course they ripped her apart in court and I should hope so too made her look like the common tart she is but that poor lad has to live with what she's said forever no one'll ever look at him right again whether he was let off or not he's tarnished for life and all because some silly girl can't keep her knickers on and it's obvious Denise is just doing the same thing she probably read the same article I did for a start if that really happened to her why didn't she tell the police straight away why did she live a lie all that time you can't credit it can you the biggest giveaway is Lil herself I mean if she really thought her daughter had been raped she wouldn't just sit back and let them get away with it and she certainly wouldn't go around telling all and sundry that's what happened if it was my child I'd get the bastard and no mistake but have they reported it have they hell and do you know why because there's nothing to report that's why they know it and everyone else knows it so I don't know why they keep on spreading all this malicious gossip people like that make me sick they really do the only one I do feel sorry for out of all this is that little baby poor little beggar born into this world not knowing who its father is and not wanted by its mother it's a shame that the faults of the parents are borne out by the children but that's the way the world is I suppose I would feel sorry for that Dan but if you ask me it's his own fault there she was stringing him along all that time when she's got someone else's child growing inside her standing at an altar in front of God wearing white if you please and lying through her teeth it's disgusting I used to think she was a nice girl too but she's evil has to be to be able to say and do all the things she has done pure evil I bet he doesn't even know what day it is half the time with all what's going on and all the lies she tells him but he brings it on himself if you ask me I mean for goodness sake he's standing by her after everything that's happened you wouldn't believe it would you but I suppose he can't have any brains hanging around with her sort in the first place I wouldn't trust any of them as far as I could throw them and you see them walking around heads held high looking like butter wouldn't melt if they expect any sympathy they won't get it from me that's for bloody certain they deserve everything they get the whole stinking lot of them and that poor little bastard is going to be sent off somewhere else for someone else to deal with it's a disgrace but I'll tell you what'll be the real slap in the face is if she ever finds out about her Frank and Carol Worthington of course I'm not going to be the one to tell her after all it's none of my business but she has to be either blind or deaf not to know what went on I heard the rumours months ago I suppose I do feel a bit sorry for her about that but at the end of the day you reap what you sow and he can't have been happy well he's never out of the Labour club or one pub or another and what she ever saw in him in the first place is beyond me he always was a rotten apple mind you her own mother was found in bed with another man you know oh yes back in the war when her first husband had gone off to fight he came back one day to find her shacked up with someone else just came back and there they were in his marital bed he walked out on her straight away and then the other bloke did a runner an all so they never knew for certain who her real father was although Jim brought her up of course she's probably half American or something like all those at Burtonwood well they say that there's probably not one among them for a five mile radius that doesn't have GI blood in there somewhere and of course you know what these Americans are like

Mark watches her turn the corner into Enfield Street and runs to the end of the road. He needs to talk to her, to tell her that he won't be like any of the others; that he'll look after her and the baby, help out with money and everything. He knows he's messed up his exams but he doesn't care. Why should he? They can't help him at the end of the day, they don't earn money for anyone. A job earns money. He was supposed to be applying to go to college after summer, but instead he's going to apply for a position at the carpet factory Jason worked in that time, a proper full time job, not a temporary thing where they can just sack you whenever they feel like it. He's going to earn his own money, buy a car, settle down with Tracy and their kid. All the others can stick college and university and all the rest of it. What would he do at college anyway? You don't need A levels to work where he wants to. He has no idea where he's going to start when he tells her, what bit to say first. Should he say he's prepared to marry her, to support her through the pregnancy, the birth and everything after that? Or should he say that he'll help out as her boyfriend, that he just wants to be a part of her life and the baby's? He peers around the corner and sees her heading up the street towards the Post Office. He thinks she shouldn't be wandering around like this in her state. Maybe that's what he should say first.

He's supposed to be going into school next month to pick up his results but he isn't going to bother. There's no point. He probably passed a few, any fool could pass for God's sake, but it won't make a difference to him whatever he gets. They said in the jobcentre that the position didn't require any qualifications or experience, that they'd teach him on the job, so what does a piece of paper matter to him now anyway? Besides, he doesn't want to see anyone from school. Not Alison, not Sam, not anyone. They'll all be running around like headless chickens trying to find out who got what, some of them happy and patting each other on the back, some of them sloping off unnoticed to cry at home. He's done with pieces of paper. He's going to get involved in the real world, with a job, money, a car, a baby. Everyone else does it and with a family of his own he can feel a part of something, be accepted, have a real purpose, not some half-arsed, unimportant tangle of dreams.

He doesn't write poetry anymore and threw away all the rubbish he'd written beforehand. His final exam had made him realise what a waste of time it all was. He had been taught to pass exams, that was all. He hadn't actually learned anything. If he'd studied and remembered what his teachers had told him then he could probably have got away with it, maybe even managed a few top grades, but what was the point? He knew, sitting in that English exam, staring down at Keats' inexplicable words, that none of it was important, none of it could help him get through life. So he could have gone to college and studied more, so what? He couldn't get a job reading poetry, didn't want a job where he had to speak French or know maths or science. All of it was a load of bollocks.

The only thing that made sense now was following Tracy, catching up to her and telling her that he had plans for them both. He was ready for a life of work and bills and babies and living away from home. That was his main priority now, earning enough money so he could move out and get on with life away from his parents. Things might be better at home than they were before, Dan was back on the scene, Denise wasn't crying, his dad had a job, but that wasn't the point anymore, he needed his own space. He watched as Tracy went into the Post Office and turned his back to lean against the house nearest him. An old woman came to her window and he saw the curtains push aside as she looked out at him, but he just stared back at her for a few moments before looking away again. He didn't care what anyone thought of him. That had been his problem in the first place, worrying about what other people thought, whether or not his parents were proud of him. They never approved of his studies anyway and now he had given them up he didn't need anything from them. If he talked to his mum she'd probably say how happy she was that he'd decided to get his life into gear, but he just wasn't interested. Now it was all about him and Tracy and the baby and everyone else could go to hell.

His back tensed up as she came out of the Post Office and started walking towards him. He didn't think she'd seen him as she was staring at the floor while she walked. She glanced up just before she was about to pass him and looked surprised to see him there. He smiled and walked beside her, feeling a bit uneasy about the situation, but knowing it had to be done sooner rather than later. He'd spent too much time wasting his life away as it was, now it was time to take some positive action.

'How's things?'

'Shit as usual. What are you doing, hanging about the street for?'

'I was waiting for you.'

'Why?'

'I wanted to talk to you.'

'Why?'

'I've had a few things on my mind since what happened on New Year's. Mainly you really. I've been thinking about you a lot. Especially considering how you are now and everything, expecting and stuff.'

'What the fuck are you on about Mark?'

'I just wanted you to know that I'm ready to look after you. I know I've only just finished school and everything, but I'm not going to bother going to college. I've decided to get a job, been down the jobcentre and everything. I want to look after you. I know things haven't been easy for you with the other ones, but I want you to know it won't be like that with me. I want to be involved, look after you and the kid when it comes.'

'Have you been dropping pills or something?'

'No, I've never felt better in my life.'

'So you're saying you want to look after me and the baby, be a dad sort of thing. What are you going to do, marry me?'

'Well we'd have to talk about it. Maybe, if that's what you wanted.'

'Mark, do you think you're the only person I fucked over Christmas? I've been to the hospital, had all the tests done. I got pregnant on Boxing Day.'

'Boxing Day? What do you mean?'

'Go away little boy. It's not yours.'

They've sacked him. He can't believe it, another job down the drain. He'd only had a day off but his boss reckons someone saw him walking into a pub when he was supposed to be suffering from flu. The truth is it had been another bleak Wednesday morning and he simply couldn't face going into work, having woken up with the sudden realisation that he had lost his best friend and the only girl he'd even thought about marrying. He managed to block it out most of the time, going round to see Craig instead of Johnny, thinking about work and work alone when in the warehouse. But that day everything had just hit him when his eyes finally opened. He looked at the alarm clock and had a moment of intense sorrow, watching the digital figures click by and counting his life down to nothingness. So he called in and said he was sick, spent the day doing nothing. He'd had to leave the house when it became too much to bear sitting on the sofa with Denise, not saying anything, both of them with their attention fixed furiously on the television screen, trying to ignore the fact that there was no longer any crying coming from the cot in the corner. She didn't move even when the phone started ringing and the blank, vacant stare in her eyes when he turned to see if she was going to do anything about the noise made him stand up and go for a drive. He went to The Navigation down by the canal, sitting alone with a pint in his hand, and watched two men further up the bank wait by rods reaching out into the murky green water. After only a few minutes it all became too depressing though, so he drank up and went into town instead.

Even the constant stream of alcohol hadn't had its usual effect on him and he'd spent the day in total misery. He didn't know that someone had seen him, but he was spotted going into the Swan and Railway at about four o'clock. He said he'd wanted some whisky for medicinal purposes, but his boss was having none of it. He's had too many days off this month already and it was beginning to take the piss. And just like that his job's gone. He spent the remainder of Thursday in bed, trying to work out who grassed him up, conjuring up visions of vengeance against the guilty party, but even that hadn't made the time go any faster. On Friday he goes into town again, officially to visit the job-centre, but in the back of his mind he is well aware that is the last place he wants to be. He has a few drinks and they help for a while, sitting in solace at the bar while he watches the assortment of people come and go. The only place he'd ever really drunk in on a weekday before was the Pagefield so he always thought it was mainly old, retired men or shabby looking drunks that occupied pubs in the afternoon. But around Wigan there is a diverse menagerie drinking in the day. The weekend feeling can be felt as early as lunchtime, and Jason sinks into the world of pub interiors quickly.

At two o'clock, when the workers have filtered back to their offices, all that remains is the core group of drinkers gathered in Harry's Bar. It is the women that interest Jason the most. He has encountered countless men sinking pint after pint in the confines of daytime beer fog in the past, with heavy guts resting against wooden bars, large arses precariously perched on high stools. He never imagined there would be women in these places too, with dank hair and dark eyes, skinny arms hidden by large padded jackets. The uniform extends to black leggings and greyed, fraying trainers, usually accompanied by a plastic supermarket shopping bag as an accessory. Cigarettes with golden rings around the tips, so long they droop, dangle from their mouths, while a golden half glass rests in one heavily ringed hand. They speak with thick accents and deep, smoky voices, while their open mouths show black gaps between grey teeth. Every now and then they erupt with cackling, coughing laughter, ultimately drowned by another swig. And, as Jason piles drink upon drink, managing a wry smile as he moves onto whisky for medicinal purposes, these languid hags take on a kind of deranged, dangerous sexuality. The gaps between their teeth become inviting, arousing the possibility of a gummy blow job, their skinny hands begin to look elegant, perched as they are on thin, wrinkled wrists. He begins to imagine talking to one of these women, buying them drinks, surely it couldn't take much to get them home, hear their dusky Dietrich voices ordering him to move harder, faster.

His growling stomach brings his thoughts out of the haze of the bar room and back to the day at hand. He stumbles from the pub and haphazardly makes his way to the nearest chippy, squinting as the daylight overwhelms him now that he has left the darkened cave. People walk around doing their usual things, carrying assorted bags, running to catch buses. Rows of them file out of North Western station to hail taxis or reclaim their cars from the car park. Jason looks at his watch and sees it's nearly half-five, absently wondering where the time has gone. Now that he is outside again, time resumes its normal journey, lives continue. Back in the pub it was a different world, obeying separate rules of time and order. Without being able to see the movement out in the street, people coming and going, the sun ticking the time by, it is easy to forget where and even who you are. It's the real world that seems a foreign place as he walks awkwardly back up the street with chips and gravy in a polystyrene tray. He pulls chip after chip out, blowing on the gravy to cool them after the first few bites have burned his tongue. The burning brings out another feeling in him, and that is to see Nicola. He walks unsteadily up past Wallgate station, past King Street, towards the corner of Library Street, where the bank is. He waits by the alleyway running to the Parish Church in the hope that he can watch her without her spotting him. He wants desperately to see her, knowing he won't be able to talk, but just wanting to look at her again. It feels like a lifetime since he has last seen her and he begins to ache with the memory.

Fifteen minutes pass before she emerges from the front door, looking to the left and right before stepping onto the street. He watches as she lets her hair down from the pony tail it was in, flicking the strands out until they rest on her shoulders. She is wearing a blue suit with a white blouse underneath. Jason's eyes are riveted by her breasts and he wonders which bra she has on, wanting to undress her, wanting for it to be his right to undress her again. She is obviously waiting for someone and Jason begins to wish it was him, as it had been just months before, when he used to call her on the phone and she would answer him gladly, whispering obscenities down the line, telling him she loved him.

But as Jason stands and watches he sees another bloke walk up and kiss her, putting his arms around her waist, drawing her up to his mouth, her hand stretching out and stroking his dark hair. And then she's gone, walking back down Library Street, hand in hand with him, leaving Jason behind, closing the door to him forever. His eyes remain fixed on the space she has just occupied, his hand absently spearing the chip tray with his wooden fork before dropping it to the floor. He starts to walk from the alleyway, having to change step quickly and put his hand out to avoid colliding with a bin. But oblivion has been a great friend to him today, he can even watch Nicola walk away with another bloke and it doesn't seem that important, his mind and body protected by a glow of drunkenness. He makes up his mind to continue this feeling, setting his feet one after the other in the direction of Scholes.

Denise sat back in the living room and exhaled a plume of grey smoke. She picked up the remote control and flicked through a few channels but there was nothing on, nothing worth watching at least. She was happy to be alone anyway. Sitting with Jason the other day, the embarrassed silence, the absolute lack of anything to say, had been hard to take. She wanted to talk to him, wanted to say something, get back to how they were years ago, before everything had somehow spiralled downwards out of control. But they had not managed one word between them, as though they were strangers, before he had eventually left her on her own again.

She longed to go back to when they were kids, when she had looked up to her older brother and doted on her younger one. She envied the children she saw playing in the street, blissfully unaware that they were part of a circle they would find near impossible to break out of. She knew her mum had been pregnant young with Jason and she had fallen into the same trap, only worse. She wished she could curl up in her dad's arms the way she used to when she was a little girl, but her respect for him has long since dissipated. It was as though none of them knew how to interact anymore. When they used to sit in front of the telly as children they would squabble and push each other, wanting to watch exactly the opposite thing the other did, with Mark just a baby playing on the carpet beneath them. But now Mark was older, out somewhere again, and she and Jason either didn't have any words to say to each other or didn't know how to form them. It was as though they had slipped into some sort of resigned, mute acceptance. There was no argument, no comment at all, when she changed channels now, the silence only broken by the man commentating on the golf. Jason had not said a word even when he had stood up and walked out of the house, the door closing behind him as definite as it could be.

And so she had continued to sit there that day, and the next day, and this day, watching innumerable pointless programmes on gardens or houses, soap operas and chat shows and game shows, waiting for Dan to come home. There were a couple of Chicken

Kievs and chips in the oven for when he got back and they'd probably go to the pub later, or maybe just rent a video and watch it with her mum and a bottle of wine. She was expecting again, although she hadn't told Dan. She wondered if maybe she should feel different about it, excited or something, but it was not that easy when she didn't know how he'd react. She hoped to God he'd be happy because she wanted to keep it, she was ready this time, ready for the responsibility and the new life they'd have. He'd put in an offer on a house in Highfield and now they were waiting to see if it would be accepted. They had had a look round it, a little semi on Kinlet Road, big enough for the two of them and a little one easily. She reached down to the table by her legs and picked up the television guide, noticing the college application forms underneath but paying no attention to them. It wasn't a priority anymore, although it still remained an idea. Maybe it would happen, maybe it wouldn't. Right now, she'd be happy just looking after the house and the baby while Dan worked.

She didn't think about it any more. The other one. It was gone now. There was no more crying in the house, no more waking up in the middle of the night to hear her mother tending to it. The adoption agency had been desperate for kids and had taken it away far sooner than she thought would have been possible. She wondered if she was heartless because she had never said goodbye, and she would never see it again, never know what might become of her child, however it had come into this world. But she repeated to herself, under her breath, 'It's not there, it's not mine, it's nothing to do with me anymore'. That part of her life had gone and she never wanted to think about it ever again. It had gone to some other family to be looked after and if it was lucky it would even be loved. She had not been able to look at it, never mind after it. She did at first, when Dan had gone and accusing eyes were focused on her all the time. She had stared at its face, trying somehow to see the face of the person who had done this to her superimposed onto the features of the child. But there had been nothing, no trace left behind, and very little of her either. And that made it easier to accept that the baby was not hers, would never be hers. She had gone through the motions, she had pushed it screaming and shiny from her body, but the moment they had cut the cord all her ties to it had been severed. She was not a mother now, she was just Denise again, the same person she had always been. No ties, apart from those she was going to reaffirm with her husband. She didn't feel hatred for who had done this to her anymore. The only thing in her mind was to get Dan back, to get her life back on track again. The baby would no longer exist in their lives, she was determined not to let it.

Her mum had not understood why she wouldn't go to the police, neither had Dan. She had kept her reasons fiercely hidden and now they accepted it. She didn't want to admit to them why she wanted to maintain her silence; that she didn't want to know who the father was because she didn't want to know anything more about it. If they found him he might say she was willing, tell everyone how she had acted, how she had consented, and then everything would be even worse. Her dad had been the most upset by it all, but he daren't say a word against her. Not after she told him she knew about New Year's Eve, how she had seen him and Carol on his bed. That had finally freed her from her father's control once and for all. He had barely looked at her, except with scorn, since they returned from the hospital. Then late one night she had come downstairs to get something to drink and he had been sitting at the dinner table with a bottle of whisky by his side. He'd stunk of alcohol and had let her have it, right then and there, about how she wasn't his daughter anymore, that he couldn't be a father to a slag. And so she'd turned on him. The man she had respected the most in her entire life became the subject of everything welling up inside her, the shame, the anger, the pain, the hatred. She told him never to speak to her again unless he wanted Mum to know about his sordid little affair. She said if he ever said anything, one word, to her about the baby ever again, she would let everyone know what kind of a man he was. People were talking anyway, and while her mum was keeping a cloak of self-deception around her, if she was to speak out, she would be believed and then everything would be out in the open.

He had started crying long before she said the words that had been building up inside her since the day he deserted her in the delivery room: 'Dad, I hate you'. Then she had gone back upstairs and he had barely spoken to her since, unless it was strictly necessary. He had stood there impassive when she told her mum that she had been raped. That she had gone to a party and woken up and known what had happened, but not who with, and she didn't think with her consent. And after her mum's tears had fallen down her face, imploring her to tell the police, tell them what she had just told her, she had broken her silence on the subject only once, to say that she wanted the baby out of her life, given away, taken out of this house and out of her sight forever. Dan had been the same, disbelief turning to sorrow and then anger. But when she had told him she was going to give the baby away, that she wanted nothing to do with it, he had slowly come around, said he would stand by her, said if she could forget then so could he. Now the baby was gone it would never be talked about again.

She hadn't realised how strong her desire to survive was before all this had happened. She cannot just lie to herself, she can make a lie true in her own mind and that is the most powerful thing of all. She will not just forget, it will never have happened: the party, the pregnancy, the birth. Everything they bought or she took will have all been for this baby, their baby. And he will paint the smaller room in their new house blue and the cot will be moved and she will go on unabashed and unashamed.

He phoned the school in the end. His mum made him. He hadn't wanted to, didn't care, and for once it was his mum who compelled him to do something about his education, so he'd called them. It turned out he hadn't failed, at least, not as spectacularly as he'd led himself to believe. He got six GCSEs in the end, five C's and even a B in history. English Literature went down the pan and he was glad he hadn't gone into school to collect his results or he might have bumped into Mrs Jameson, his English teacher. He could imagine the look of disappointment on her face without having to actually see it. French went, as did geography, but what did he care? With six GCSEs he could easily follow the path he'd marked out for himself. It mightn't include Tracy and a child anymore, but it certainly didn't involve carrying on at school, his first pay cheque had convinced him of that. He used to be made up when he got ten quid down the Parish Hall for collecting glasses and now he was earning proper money he was addicted. Any overtime that was going begging he was the first in line to volunteer. He was the only one out of him, Jason and Denise to have a proper job, and he'd ended up doing better than both of them in his exams as well. He feels he has escaped and that is all that matters, escaped being different, escaped being sidelined and ostracised and joked about. His mum now gives him a chicken leg at tea, the most encouragement, the biggest smiles.

In a way he is disappointed about what happened with Tracy, but relieved as well. He could still be fertile and he doesn't have to deal with any extra responsibility, at least, not for now. He can go to work and out at the weekend and get pissed and meet girls all under the guise of normality. The only concession he makes to this is his reading. Free from the constraints of school, the methods of learning, he reads and reads. He does not need to worry about exams and how he should interpret what is on the page, but can lose himself for a few hours in something different, exotic, exciting. He finished *Lord of the Flies* and is reading it again. Sitting in the canteen at work, he makes his way through the pages while devouring sweet tea and tuna sandwiches. Most of the others in the factory read newspapers: The Sun, The Mirror, The Express, while the well-read make their way through The Daily Mail. But though he reads his books, he is not considered different like he was at school. Reading is reading in here and everyone does it to some extent. Besides, he takes his dinner later than most, at one, by which time the canteen is almost deserted, the fat women in greasy chequered aprons clank plates together in soapy washing up bowls behind the empty counter that had been overrun less than an hour earlier.

He still imagines himself on the island when he reads, not as Piggy anymore, but with war paint and a loin cloth, carrying a spear and chasing Ralph through the fire. He still sees himself on foreign shores, he wants to travel, to see the sun set over the sea, mist form around mountains, but, unlike before, he is also happy where he is. Wigan has everything he needs and pretty soon he'll find a decent bird, a fit one, and take her to Blackpool or Southport on a weekend, walk along the seafront, shag in woods. He still watches Stacey from time to time, but not with the uniform regularity of old. These days he's either down the pub or the park, drinking with the lads, laughing with the girls. Coarse hair is starting to accumulate on his top lip and he has to brush his mum aside when she grabs his cheek, proud he'll soon be shaving properly. Everything is looking up as far as he is concerned. Never before has he really been treated as an equal until now. He laughs at the jokes his workmates tell him, goes with them for a few pints in the Cherry Gardens when his shift ends. Only the bus ride home reminds him he has still not achieved his primary goal. One of the blokes from work lets him drive his car every now and then though and he reckons he'll nearly be ready for his test by the time he turns seventeen. But it seems so far away and that is his only complaint, that he cannot move time on to his eighteenth birthday, when he will have everything he wants, legitimate pub entry, although he rarely gets stopped now anyway, a car and a girlfriend. For the meantime he has to bite his tongue, put his money into a bank account, and wait.

The job is easy enough, as was getting it. Just days after he'd been to the jobcentre and found what he was looking for he'd had an interview and they'd taken him on. The man had looked suspicious of him at first, his predicted grades looked too good, but Mark had convinced him they'd been overestimated. He had pressed Mark as to whether or not he was certain he wanted this job, would stick at it, not just look for something different when he got bored and wanted to move on.

'You could get a job in the offices with grades like these.'

'I don't want a job in the offices, I want to use my hands, I want to get involved.'

His answers had obviously impressed as he'd been given the

job on the spot and started work the Monday after. The weekend before he celebrated out round town, most of the time able to get into all the pubs, not just the ones that let people in regardless of age. He didn't bother with Cheers anymore, but went to the Walkabout and Springbok, drinking bottles and grabbing girls on the dance floor. More often than not it worked too and he was usually attached to someone's face by the end of the night. Saturdays are the same, while on Sundays he just hangs around the house, sitting and reading, the telly on in the background, undisturbed in a way he'd never been when he'd been at school. He looked up from his book when he heard his supervisor call out to him from the doors leading to the factory floor, the noise from the machines and his barking voice bringing him back into the canteen.

'Hey Shag! You'll fuck your eyes up reading like you do. If you spent as much time working as you did reading that bleeding book you might get summat done. Just 'cos it's Friday doesn't mean you can slack off. Five minutes and I want you back out here, there's a mountain of fucking cardboard building up.'

Jason sat back on the burn-hole cratered brown sofa and inhaled deeply. The room was filled with blue smoke and he wiped his eyes when water started streaming down his cheek after he blinked some in. He hadn't been back here for ages but thankfully John had remembered who he was, let him in, given him some gear, even offered credit when he realised he didn't have much money left on him after his time down the pub. Fortunately for Jason too, John told him all about his dog Tyson having to be put down after it attacked one of the kids from a nearby estate in a park.

'Kid needed surgery. I blame the parents, letting their kids run wild around dogs. I know a bloke who can get another one though, an American fighting dog.'

Jason had only remembered the bull mastiff after knocking on the door. He'd been allowed inside, walking in and scouring the flat for the beast as he did so, and his anxiety was only allayed when John told him of Tyson's demise. There were two others gathered at the flat, smoking pot and watching telly, and Jason was introduced to Greg and Rachel, who grunted their hellos back at him. Jason's head was spinning out of control as all the alcohol caught up with him, but he was happy to wallow in the feeling, a feeling of emptiness, where no memory of his job or Nicola or his life could attack him.

If time had slowed in the pubs in Wigan, then it stopped completely in the flat itself. The passing of the day could not even be noted by what TV programme was on next as they were watching a DVD, *Predator*, and Jason and the others grinned as Arnie and his army mates ran around the jungle bare-chested, shooting at the alien thing after them. John hadn't even looked surprised to see Jason when he had arrived, just let him in, waved away his embarrassment at his lack of funds, saying he could have a bit on spec, pay him back some other time. They were chilling out in anticipation of the night ahead, when they were going to pop some pills and go to The Pier, and Jason was glad they had other plans as it meant he could slope away when they went to the club, make his excuses and stagger back home where he could finally find refuge in sleep. He felt tired now, but somehow managed to keep his eyes open to watch the film as soldier after soldier was picked off in front of him.

He had done what he wanted to do, forget about things for a while, step outside of his life for a few hours, fill his body with mind-numbing substances, and for brief moments he even felt happy. Greg and Rachel, sitting beside him, were placid from smoking, while John flitted around, getting ready for the night ahead, wearing jeans but nothing else, showing off his array of tattoos and gym-toned torso. He had a knife in his hand like the one Arnie was using in the film, carrying it with him as a sort of nervous habit, the blade glinting as the setting sun intermittently shone through the far window. John didn't work, didn't have to, his dealing had no doubt paid for his hi-tech stereo system and wide screen TV, while the council sorted out his rent. He was in a hyper mood, totally contrasted by the lethargy on the couch, and when a knock came on the door he jumped up and opened it sharply, pushing the knife towards whoever was outside. Jason looked over and saw Tariq in the doorway, laughing at John, but pushing the knife so it pointed away from him. He smiled when he saw Jason and sat on the arm of the couch next to him.

'All reet Jay.'

'All reet Tariq, how's it going mate?'

'Can't complain you know. Give us a drag on that.'

'I will if you give us one of them bottles.'

'Fucking hell, I've only got four. Here, fuck it, have one. What are you doing here anyway?'

'He just turned up on my doorstep, didn't you mate? Wanted a bit of weed,' said John, moving around the room, stabbing his knife at imaginary adversaries.

'Fair enough. How's your sister doing?' said Tariq, opening one of his remaining three bottles.

'She's all right, considering,' said Jason, turning away from Tariq for the first time and watching the film.

'I've not seen your Denise since the party I had here ages ago, what's she been doing?' said John, finally sitting down in an armchair to Jason's right.

'She got married and stuff. Had a kid.'

'Yeh, I heard about that. I can't believe she got rid of it man, that's well out of order,' said John.

'Well she couldn't look after it on her own and Dan wasn't going to stick about if she kept it.'

'He's a cunt that lad,' said Tariq.

'Dan's all right. I wouldn't want to look after a kid that wasn't mine. I thought he was your mate anyway?' Jason said.

'He's no mate of mine.'

Jason wanted to change the subject and was grateful when John called Tariq into the kitchen. He didn't like talking about what had happened to his sister with anyone. He supposed it was because at home they never talked about it, silence was the only way to deal with it as far as he was concerned. Jason thought Tariq seemed to have the same attitude towards talk of him and

Dan being mates and he supposed maybe they'd fallen out the way he and Johnny had. Nothing surprised him anymore.

Tariq came back into the living room, drinking from one of the bottles he had brought with him, using the beer to swallow what was no doubt a pill, possibly two. Jason had never tried ecstasy and didn't want to. He knew with his luck he'd be one of those people he'd seen in the paper, dead, with the headline something like: 'First Time Ecstasy User Dies'. He'd heard it talked about, especially by people like Tariq and John, and he didn't think he could take being out of control in the way they always described it. Being drunk and stoned he could handle, you knew where you stood, and although John probably wouldn't give him anything dodgy, even he might not know what was in his pills half the time. Tariq sat back down on the edge of the sofa before moving next to Jason when Greg went with John into the kitchen. They talked about Arnie and the film, laughing at his one-liners, his dodgy accent and acting. After a while he started to get restless though, just as Jason was beginning to settle in. He turned the film off and put some music on instead.

It was exactly the sort of music Jason didn't like when he'd been drinking, the kind that drilled into your head, with no lyrics that an addled brain could grab onto and hold, like a crutch that helped you keep a slight grasp on sobriety. Instead, the incessant banging and deep bass notes made his bones vibrate and his stomach churn and when he couldn't take it anymore he stood up to go to the toilet.

He wanted to go home, but when he flushed the toilet and turned to leave, he knew he was going to throw up. Jason hadn't been properly sick since he was about seventeen and his judgement of when it was about to come was so mistimed that he missed the toilet entirely. He managed to turn halfway through and aimed the rest into the wash basin. He heard clamouring behind him and someone shouting and someone laughing. When he finally finished, he wiped his mouth and turned to see John and Tariq standing in the doorway.

'You'd better fucking clean that up,' said John. 'What is it with your family that you always have to fucking puke in my bathroom?'

Jason turned to look at the mess he had made and was nearly sick again. When he was at last sure there was no more to come, he turned on the tap to wash out the basin before leaning over and having a drink. He felt a lot more sober than he had earlier but his head was still all over the place. John passed him a cloth and he got down on his hands and knees to clean the carpet and the rim of the bowl where some had splattered. It was mostly liquid and the smell was terrible, and as he wrung the cloth into the toilet he heard John and Tariq talking behind him.

'So have you got any roofies for tonight?' Tariq was saying.

'I told you mate, it's been quiet on that score for ages now, no one's got any anywhere. You had the last I had at my party,' said John. 'You'll just have to try and pull the normal way.'

'Fuck you, normal way. I can pull, don't worry about that. It was fucking great last time, that's all.'

'What was so great about it? She won't have known what the fuck she was doing.'

'Denise knew what she was doing man, she's always wanted a bit of me.'

'Suit yourself T. I don't care what you say about it, I still can't believe you shagged her after she'd thrown up.'

'I made her brush her teeth first, what do you think I am, stupid?' Tariq said.

'No I think you're a dirty cunt.'

'She's the one with the dirty cunt mate, not me,' said Tariq. Jason heard them both start to laugh.

Somewhere deep inside Jason's blancmanged brain the words he was hearing were slowly being processed and understood. He could see his sister, could remember something she had told him about a party at John's flat, could hear John and Tariq laughing. He looked down at the carpet as he continued to scrub and the unexpected words that came from his mouth were those he thought he could only hear inside his head.

'You saw my sister at that party?'

'Yeh,' said Tariq between fading giggles.

'You saw her at that party,' Jason repeated, his mind still working the words and thoughts he was voicing.

'Is there a fucking echo in here or something?' said Tariq, laughing again. Something clicked with Jason, a significance to what he was hearing that he was having trouble to grasp properly. Deep within his brain a memory popped up out of nowhere. He remembered once sitting through a talk at school some nurse was giving, about the dangers for girls leaving drinks unattended in clubs when they went dancing. About how it was usually someone you knew.

'Roofies?' Jason said. 'Fucking roofies?'

'You'd better watch your mouth boy, this isn't your business,' said John.

'Not my business? That's my fucking sister you're talking about,' said Jason, finally turning to Tariq in anger.

His senses were so numbed that he barely moved even when he realised what was going to happen. Tariq lunged forward and landed a foot squarely into his face, knocking his head back onto the porcelain of the toilet. His eyes closed involuntarily as a searing pain ripped through his scalp before he felt hands grabbing at him, pulling him out of the bathroom. He felt a punch hit the side of his head and he staggered backwards, desperate not to go down now that it had started, knowing that if he went down he could be in serious trouble. Years ago he had gone to ground to try and appease the guy hitting him, hoping his prone position would make him stop, but it had enraged him even further and the subsequent kicks he received meant he had his ribs bandaged for weeks afterwards after two were broken. He knew his only chance to survive was to fight back but as he went to lash out he felt someone kick him in the back of his legs. He stumbled into Tariq and grabbed onto him for balance, but his vision went black a moment later as Tariq's head smashed into his own. Unbearable pain went through his nose and he finally fell to his knees. His hands went up to protect his face, but his fingers slid off as they were covered in blood. He looked down and saw it pouring from his face onto his shirt before another kick from behind sent him sprawling headfirst onto the carpet. He moved into a foetal position as he was kicked again and again, the blows arching his back one minute, sprawling him outwards the next. All of a sudden they stopped and he felt himself being lifted from the floor, hoping that would signal an end to the assault. His right eye was half closed but he could see he was being taken over to the door. He flinched as sly punches landed in his side and his face before the door was opened and his feet were lifted from the ground. He looked at the stairwell for a moment before he was thrown into it, only landing halfway down, his body twisting as he hit the steps, his arms and legs bending unnaturally as he bounced to the concrete slab of the next flight. He curled up as pain wracked his body from the inside out, burning through him. He heard the door close above him before all that was left were the drum beats from before, the volume turned up so high that the stairwell physically moved, pounding through his head like the end of the world.

'Two and three, twenty-three. Four and five, forty-five. On its own, number nine.'

Denise felt the burden of her knowledge, sitting there in the red room listening to the bingo caller, trying to keep her attention on the rectangular piece of card in front of her. She knew she was probably missing numbers all over the place, but she couldn't concentrate no matter what. Her mind was fixed on how she was going to tell Dan and her mum about the new baby.

She looked up at them for a brief moment to see they were blissfully ignorant of her inner struggle. Dan was absently looking over to the bar, evidently wondering whether or not he should get another pint now or wait until the others had finished, while her mum was fixated on the cards in front of her, ticking off numbers with an oversized marker pen. They swore blind that they believed her, despite not showing any of the signs that they did. Shouldn't there be horror, sympathy and anguish, even now, at what she had told them, at what had happened to her? Their acceptance seemed too instant, too quiet, too distant, to seem real. Not that it had been easy to win Dan back. Even with the baby gone he still made intimations towards wanting revenge when he'd had too much to drink. But her protestations and belligerence about not wanting to involve the police, not wanting to relive it all, had calmed him. Almost too much, it felt like sometimes. Now there was no pain in their eyes at what she had told them, no grief for her ordeal. It remained unspoken, passed over almost, as though it had never happened. And, although she could not have hoped for a better or smoother outcome, she felt as though she had been cheated somehow, that something was being left unsaid.

She is afraid that when she tells them she has a baby on the way, Dan's eyes will have the question of whether or not it is his behind them. It is a situation she does not want to confront and yet somehow the silence is even more eerie and unnatural. The caller finally stopped when someone shouted house from one of the tables behind her. She did not turn to see who it was, although her mum looked up in dismay at being beaten to the chase: a tray of assorted meats for the winner; a brief, forced round of applause from those who had not won and a peal of triumphant cheers from the table where the lucky woman had been sitting. Dan stood up at last and asked about drinks before heading off to get another round in. She never imagined that at eighteen her Saturdays would be spent like this, but all in all she has done well. She still has her husband, her life can go on. All she has to do now is persuade herself that she wants it to, that she is happy.

'I can't believe it, I was only two away from a house then.'

'Never mind Mum, maybe you'll win the next game.'

'How many did you get?'

'I don't know, I wasn't paying attention.'

'You might have won if you'd been listening you daft sod. What's up with you anyway? You look a bit off colour today love.'

'I just feel a bit run down that's all.'

'Well, that's to be expected I suppose. Thank you Dan love.'

That's how it always is now, however she acts is to be expected, although no one says why. Mind you, her mum's thoughts were no doubt preoccupied with Jason at the moment anyway. They'd received a phone call late last night and had gone straight to the hospital to see him. He'd been in a right state, although he refused to tell anyone what had happened to him. He had a broken arm, a broken nose, a black eye and a body covered in bruises and cuts. The police said they'd be back, but there was nothing they could do if Jason didn't want to talk to them. Denise had tried to talk to him, but even though she felt she knew what he was going through, she still didn't know what to say. Her mum had cried and her dad had been angry and it reminded her all too much of another time. Jason said he was going to look for a job when he felt well enough, although everyone told him not to be daft, that he needed rest and time to recover. Then Denise told him she'd seen Nicola round town and that she'd asked about him. She felt even worse about lying when she saw the glimmer of hope in his eyes at the mention of her name. Her mum had been to see him that morning as well and they were all going later when visiting hours were on in the evening.

She knew it wouldn't be hard for him to get a job though, it hadn't taken her two minutes when she'd got round to it. There'd been loads of vacancies down the jobcentre and she'd managed to get some cleaning work at Pemberton High starting next week so she'll be able walk down to work on a morning and be finished by nine o'clock. The money wasn't fantastic, but added to Dan's wage they'd get by well enough. Mark seemed made up in his job, she was back in work, her mum was at the Hospice, so all it needed now was her dad and Jason to get themselves sorted and things might be able to return to normal again. Whatever had happened in the past could be forgotten and they could go along as they had before, except with her and Dan set up in their own place. Dan reckoned his offer on the house in Highfield would be accepted any day now and then they'd be able to move straight in. Denise couldn't wait for that, and thought maybe she should hang on until they'd got their own place before telling Dan she was pregnant. But then, while the club was quiet apart from people milling about buying new cards and getting ready for the next game, she had a sudden feeling that it was the right moment. She knew her mum was worried about Jason but too many things had been kept hidden and glossed over in the past and it had got everyone nowhere. She was going to seize the moment, tell them right then, and with the rising excitement tinged with fear inside her, she hadn't realised Dan had seen the concentration on her face.

'What's up wi' you at all? You've looked like you've had summat on your mind since we came in here.'

'I have got something on my mind. Dan, Mum, I need to tell you both something.'

'Well tell us then, before we all die of old age.'

'I'm pregnant. Dan's got me pregnant.'

The silence was deadly and her heart dropped as she began to think her timing was all wrong. She looked to Dan to see if he was apprehensive but couldn't see his face as he looked at her mum. Her mum's face at first gave nothing away, but then Dan turned to her and she saw the broad smile before his arms engulfed her and she nearly couldn't breathe through the squeeze he gave her. She looked up to see her mum's face light up as well now that Dan's reaction was good. She closed her eyes and clung to Dan's arm, feeling as though she wouldn't be able to stop smiling. Everything could be complete now, house, husband, baby. The words spun around inside her head as her mum kissed her heavily on the cheek, wiping away the lipstick she left behind afterwards.

'This calls for a celebration. Dan, get the drinks in.'

'I've just got 'em in.'

'Well get some more in, we've got to celebrate! Orange juice for our Denise though.'

'Mum!'

'Oh all right, get her what she wants. Here, take this.'

'Cheers Lil. Drinks all round then.'

Frank sits in the stands at the JJB watching Latics. He's been watching the same team since he was a little kid brought in by his dad, although of course back then it was at Springfield Park. He sees the players kicking the football about, toiling away, trying to get an edge over the other team. It's Wycombe Wanderers this week so the away support isn't much to talk about, the Wigan lads outsinging them easily. Frank doesn't shout too much when he's at the match. He joins in with the songs he knows and every now and then calls out in encouragement, but most of the time he just sits and studies the proceedings on the pitch, watching the movement, wondering what tactics need to be employed to win the game. The ball swings from one side of the halfway line to the other, never venturing very near either penalty area, most of the time being headed back and forth. 'Get bloody thing on ground!' someone sitting next to him shouts out. It's not much of a match today, a mid-table clash with neither team really optimistic about making the play-offs or seemingly of even winning the game in progress. Frank thinks he should shout more, voice his support louder, let the lads know he's behind them, but there isn't much to shout about, the battle long and drawn out in the middle of the park, little goalmouth action of note and chances, when they come, are invariably squandered. What's the point in shouting and getting all worked up when the game isn't even a good one?

He begins to think that life, like football, is just a game at the end of the day. Both have their ups and downs, their moments of glory and tears, moments of dazzling skill and costly own goals. Latics have always been something of a middling team, even the road up to the Second Division, and the time before when it had officially been the third, had been a long and taxing one. The players put in the effort, they go out week after week trying to advance themselves up the league table, but at the end of the season they ultimately never go up or down. He's lost count of the amount of times they've lost out in the play-offs after missing the automatic promotion spots, or other times when they've narrowly avoided relegation. In recent years they have just stayed constant, neither brilliant nor consigned to an even lower league. It's depressing in many ways and Frank has wondered in the past why he bothers watching at all when he can pretty much bet on what the end result will be: middle-of-the-road. He knows blokes who support Man United or Liverpool, who have seasons of FA Cup runs or league success, real highs and lows, and mainly highs. Not like Latics, not like his life. He thought of the time, years ago, when he'd gone to a casino and played blackjack. He'd been up something like a hundred pound, raking in the money, hand after hand going his way. Of course he lost it all, bet it all back until he was fifty down. Three hours later and he'd recouped his losses until he'd left the place with just enough money for one last drink.

But that was what it was all about. As long as you have enough to make you happy, why would you want anything more? He had three kids, a wife and a house. No proper, permanent full-time job still, but that would come in time, a bloke down the pub told him all about some work going the other day, and for decent money too. The Carols of the world were for other men, men who wanted their brass polished up a bit, when, with all said and done, brass was still brass. And anyway, he decided, there's always the rugby, although he had to admit that even they'd gone to pot recently. High after high had eventually been brought back down to earth with a bump, something that most of the supporters found hard to take, denial having set in to hide the disappointment. He can still remember the feeling of being at Wembley when it was the Challenge Cup final though. Year after year it was, London like a second home. Yet for some reason he's always been more drawn to Latics, to football, to twenty-two blokes battling it out on a football field, always aiming for somewhere higher and never quite getting there. You know your place, but you keep on trying anyway, otherwise what's the point? Every now and then there are jackpots to be hit, small jackpots, but jackpots all the same, and there are pitfalls to be fallen into, but you pick yourself up and keep on going.

Watching Latics had changed a lot over the years: a big new stadium; new, expensive players; hope – always hope that maybe this year will be the year that it happens. Down the pub afterwards for a few pints, to go over the game, never in minute detail, always with the bigger picture in mind: who was coming next week; how the league table was standing at the moment; rumours of transfers and new financial opportunities taken from the newspaper. The games themselves were mostly nothing to write home about but in the grand scheme of things there was always the chance that there might be better to come eventually. And the feeling of winning is too great not to take a chance on, even if you know next week you'll probably lose and you'll end up in the same place where you started.

Frank looks up suddenly as a gasp comes from the bloke next to him, a buzz beginning to develop across the stand as the voices of the home support start to rise in united anticipation. When he finally focuses on what's happening down on the pitch again he can't tell exactly who's got the ball, but he sees it crossed into the penalty area. There is a melee in the eighteen yard box, the ball firing round like a pinball, shirts from both sides jostling to get to it, until finally, gloriously, it is hammered into the top of the net. Frank rises in unison with the crowd, screaming out at the top of his lungs, 'Yes!'

He might be sixteen and she might be twenty and she might have always gone out with lads very different to him in the past, but he's working now, becoming a grown up, earning his own money, so things are different, the playing field is more even. He doesn't feel like the same person he was only a year ago and in many ways he finds it hard to connect with the memories he has of how he was back then. If things can change so drastically so quickly, who can tell what will happen in the future? The weeks will go by, a few more girls will go under his belt, and all of a sudden he'll be changed again. Tracy was eighteen and he'd had her so the same thing could happen with Stacey if he put his mind to it. Admittedly she has a new bloke now, but she's always falling out with this one like she did with the one before. He's seen them arguing in the street a few times when he's come home early from town, heard them shouting at each other, and that might mean she'll need a shoulder to cry on at some point. Timing was everything in this game. That was definitely something he'd learnt. And she knew him as well, would probably be happy to talk her problems over with him. He'd hand her a bottle of beer or a glass of wine and they'd chat in her room, talking it over, him telling her, 'Don't worry, everything will work out all right.'

He longs to be inside her room, feels if that can happen the final hurdle will have been crossed. Her curtains are nearly always closed by the time he gets home these days, he's usually out somewhere until well after she's come home and gone to bed. He sees her out and about with her baby though and thinks she's never looked better than she does as a mother, never looked so womanly. Her figure had returned in no time, curves back exactly where they should be, no sign whatsoever that she's dropped a kid apart from the pram she pushes around. One of his mates told him one night about how he'd gone with an older girl, how she'd said she preferred younger lads, that they were more of a laugh, and Mark reckons Stacey is the same. She's never even got on with any of the blokes she's been with before and they've always been older, so who's to say she wouldn't be up for a bit of a change? He'd give her a change all right. He'd treat her well, take her out, look after her, pander to her every need. When he'd fancied other girls in the past he'd felt like he'd been cheating on her, or at least the idea of her. Now he believes it had all been part of a learning process, that he'd needed to go with other girls so that he'd be ready when she came calling. He knows what to do now, he's been there enough times not to have to worry about anything like that. Not like ages ago, when fumbling had been the order of the day and you took five hours getting a bra strap off.

The girl he went with last Friday, Debbie, had told him he was the best pull she'd ever had. He'd taken her down the side of Cheers after they'd left and been denied entrance to any of the other pubs. The police vans on King Street gave away why all the publicans were suddenly being so cautious. Give it two weeks and it'll be back to normal though. He'd had her up against the iron gate at the end of the alley, had her spasming against his hand as he rubbed, biting her lip as she tried to stop herself from crying out loud. He sits in his room remembering every moment, *Of Mice and Men* resting ignored in his lap. Looking out of his window he can see that she's still not back yet. It shouldn't be long now though, it's nearly teatime and she's always back for then. It's raining outside, the wispy sort of rain that you don't notice until you're soaking wet. She's out with him somewhere, he saw them leave in the car together, probably to go up to Ashurst Beacon or the Three Sisters, places Jason has told him about, places he wants to go as soon as he gets a car. The dream spurs him on, makes him work as hard as he can, refusing to fall into the trap Jason used to and getting sacked all the time. Jason had laughed when he found out the sergeant major was still at the carpet factory and said to ask him if he had enough glue, but didn't explain what it meant so Mark hasn't dared to say anything.

He sits up when he hears a car stop outside and, standing and looking down, he sees it parked across the road. He puts his book on the desk and, after checking his hair in the mirror, sets off downstairs. He's determined to talk to her, say something to her, let her know how he feels. He doesn't even care what her bloke will think about it, he's going to do something. He stands in the front yard, trying to find cover from the rain, watching as they mess about and smiling as the windows start to steam over from the inside. He's hiding behind the bushes by the side of the house, treasuring the moment, imagining it's him in the car with her. She might not have had a bump for a long time but he fantasises about what it would be like to run his hand over her stomach where it used to be, to have his mouth pressed on hers. He's wanted inside for tea, his mum yelling blue murder because Denise isn't back yet and he's nowhere to be found and that useless fuck of a husband is down the pub again, the chips are getting cold and she's got to go to the hospital later to see Jason. The car bobs about from time to time and he raises his head to see better when he hears her squeal with laughter. When they finally finish and the car drives away he walks out into the yard. She looks over and smiles at him, blowing him a kiss. He'll have her one day.

Lightning Source UK Ltd.
Milton Keynes UK
15 December 2009

147549UK00001BA/138/A

9 781905 796069